W9-CBR-925

THE
Doggy Divas
ROXY'S RULES

THE
Doggy Divas
ROXY'S RULES

LAUREN BROWN

sourcebooks
jabberwocky

Copyright © 2010 by Lauren Brown
Cover and internal design © 2010 by Sourcebooks, Inc.
Cover design by Cara Petrus
Cover illustration by Cara Petrus
Sourcebooks and the colophon are registered trademarks of Sourcebooks, Inc.

All rights reserved. No part of this book may be reproduced in any form or by any electronic or mechanical means including information storage and retrieval systems—except in the case of brief quotations embodied in critical articles or reviews—without permission in writing from its publisher, Sourcebooks, Inc.

The characters and events portrayed in this book are fictitious or are used fictitiously. Any similarity to real persons, living or dead, is purely coincidental and not intended by the author.

Published by Sourcebooks Jabberwocky, an imprint of Sourcebooks, Inc.
P.O. Box 4410, Naperville, Illinois 60567-4410
(630) 961-3900
Fax: (630) 961-2168
www.jabberwockykids.com

Library of Congress Cataloging-in-Publication data is on file with the publisher.

Source of Production: Webcom, Toronto, Ontario, Canada
Date of Production: September 2010
Run Number: 13542

Printed and bound in Canada.
WC 10 9 8 7 6 5 4 3 2 1

Dedicated to all those girls sitting in front of their laptops and daydreaming about their name on the cover of a book.

Don't give up! Those fantasies *will* become a reality! Also lots of love and special thank-yous to Nathanael for his never-ending patience, support, and motivation *and* for being the best sounding board a girl could ever ask for. And, of course, to Mom, Dad, Marc, Lindsie, and Poppop for always being my Number One fans.

ROXY DAVIS SMEARED A glob of shim.   , on her already naturally pink lips, covered u, .ier sparkly, brown eyes with a pair of oversized sunglasses, and let out a long, deep sigh.

What's taking so long? she wondered as she leaned into the leather seat cushion in the backseat of her dad's silver sports car.

Roxy couldn't imagine being late for the first day of school. She was expected to be on the front steps with the rest of her crew. It would look terrible for the queen bee of the seventh grade to get to school after the first bell rang. Well, co-queen bee.

She was sharing the honor with her best friend, Liz Craft, of course. They were the new princesses of Monroe Middle School, and they had waited all summer to wear their crowns. Liz would be ultra-annoyed if Roxy showed up even one second late. When Roxy's platinum pink BlackBerry started buzzing in her lap, her stomach knotted up like a pretzel. The text was from Liz.

Leaving in a few—what's ur location?

ver to the front seat and started pounding on
n.

"Dad!" she screamed out the window. "Dad! I'm going
to be late!"

Roxy's dad came running out of the house. His tie was
hanging loosely around his neck, and he was carrying his
suit jacket over his briefcase. He looked disheveled and
angry as he got in the driver's seat.

"Roxy, we never leave for school this early," he said
breathlessly. "And why are you in the backseat? I'm not
your chauffeur."

"C'mon, Dad, this year is way different. That means
I absolutely have to be on the front steps at *least* twenty
minutes before the first bell," she tried to explain calmly.
"And gross! Only sixth graders sit in the front seat with
their daddies!"

Roxy's dad sighed, turned on the radio, and started
singing along to a whiny old tune from the '80s. Roxy
tried to block the sound out while texting Liz a little
white lie.

Almost there!

Roxy closed her eyes and twirled her pin-straight brown
hair around her perfectly manicured finger. Hair-twirling
was her worst habit, and she only did it when she was
stressed. During sixth grade, Roxy and Liz had worked
very hard to earn the respect of their classmates—allowing

them to rise to the top of the social circle for this year. Roxy wasn't about to ruin that on the first day of school.

She tried to relax, but her skinny jeans were too tight. She squirmed and quickly unfastened the top button. *Whew*. At least she could breathe *before* school. According to the Fashion Bible—the top-secret notebook Liz and Roxy used to plan their daily outfits down to a nail-polish shade, Roxy was to complement her too-tight jeans with the perfect pair of rocket-red platform boots.

The boots already pinched her feet, but Roxy had known she was taking that risk when she'd bought them a half size too small. It wasn't so much a risk as a requirement. Liz had insisted they share shoes so they could double their wardrobe options.

Roxy didn't mind that Liz had feet a half size smaller than hers. After all, Liz had perfect arches and needed to wear properly fitting shoes at all times. Besides, once an outfit was logged into the Fashion Bible, there was no turning back.

"Holy Mother of…" Roxy's dad yelled as the car came screeching to a halt. It jerked forward so suddenly that Roxy's sunglasses flew off and her BlackBerry vanished underneath the front seat.

"Dad! Come on—I'm late…" Roxy looked out the window—and then blinked and looked again. Was she seeing things? "Dad? What's happening? What's going on?"

Traffic was backed up in every lane of the main intersection—the same intersection that Roxy needed to cross to get to school. All of the town's dog walkers marched in front of the traffic jam—with no regard for the green traffic lights. They paced back and forth with signs in their hands that read, "DOG WALKERS ON STRIKE!" They chanted in unison slogans like, "Dog Walkers Unite!"

But that wasn't the worst of it. Every dog the walkers were responsible for ran free in the streets. People were abandoning their cars in the middle of the street to search for their lost dogs. Those without dogs had no choice but to leave their cars too. The risk of running over a pooch made driving way too dangerous. The dogs, however, clearly loved every second of their newfound freedom.

"Dad! How am I going to get to school?" Roxy shrieked while an oversized black poodle started pawing at her through the window. "I should have been there already!"

Roxy's dad leaned on the horn to shoo away a Doberman that was using the hood of their car as a tanning bed.

"I hate to tell you, but I think you're going to have to walk the rest of the way, Pumpkin," her dad sighed. "It's only a few more blocks."

"I'm already late!" Roxy's voice went up three octaves. The ears of a few dogs surrounding the car perked up at the shrill noise.

"You're acting rather spoiled, Roxy," Mr. Davis said sternly. "And I don't think you have much choice about walking."

Roxy managed to locate her BlackBerry and texted Liz. This was an absolute catastrophe.

Have u seen loser dog walkers & picket line? Going 2 b late…
don't freak!

Hitting "Send," Roxy knew Liz *would* freak. She slammed
the car door shut, muttering a quick good-bye to her dad.
Taking slow, tiny steps in her too tight, too tall boots,
Roxy began to tiptoe her way through the mess of dogs
and people. She didn't want to tumble over—and walking
this slowly was the only way to prevent her feet from going
numb with pain.

Why did I ever listen to Liz? Of course, she *decided to wear
flats today! It's going to take me hours at this rate!*

"Dog Walkers on Strike!"

"Dog Walkers Unite!"

The chanting was loud and overwhelming. *Great, I'm
going to go deaf too,* Roxy worried as she navigated her way
along the messy sidewalks.

She had to watch every step while passing through the
dangerous zone of dog-pile land mines. Dogs of every size,
color, and breed ran wild through the streets. Chihuahuas
and Yorkshire terriers were playing tug-of-war with a water hose. A pack of Dalmatians and Labrador retrievers
were going from garden to garden and digging up carefully
manicured flower beds. Several fluffy sheepdogs herded
small children safely through crosswalks.

Lazy malamutes and Bernese mountain dogs slept on
sidewalks, enjoying mid-morning naps. Impressive Great
Danes planted themselves in front of shop entrances, not

allowing anyone in or out. And spunky greyhounds and border collies swiftly chased cats up trees. Roxy's usually beautiful neighborhood looked like a giant, overrun dog park.

Why isn't Liz texting me back? Roxy started to panic. She was officially late. And since Liz lived around the corner from the school, she didn't have to deal with the chaos.

Even though Roxy knew her thoughts made perfect sense, she also knew that Liz would never see it her way. If aliens abducted Roxy this morning, Liz would accuse her of being more loyal to some weird space creatures than to her.

Roxy was about to risk spraining her ankle by breaking into a full-on sprint when she felt something pulling at her leg.

"Little Roxie! What are you doing here?" Roxy squealed. Nipping at her feet was Liz's little black-and-tan Yorkie-Poo, which although spelled differently, happened to be named Roxie too. "Did those stupid dog walkers let you loose?"

Roxy picked up little Roxie. The tiny dog was shaking, but she licked Roxy's face and calmed down as soon as she felt safe. Little Roxie had already been a part of Liz's family when the girls became friends in the second grade. At first, Liz had suggested that Roxy should think about changing her name—but instead they called the cute pooch "little" Roxie. (Liz had a knack for noting Roxy's similarities with little Roxie too!)

Right now, little Roxie might just be the lucky charm

Roxy needed to turn around her morning of misfortunes. Liz couldn't blame Roxy for being a few minutes late because she had rescued little Roxie from the dog-walkers' strike. *Could she?*

Roxy breathed a sigh of relief as she and little Roxie headed up the marble steps that led to the mansion where Liz's family lived. Roxy wasn't sure if anyone was home, but she knew that the Crafts kept a spare key in the basket of flowers next to the front door, and she couldn't waste any more time getting to school.

"Now you be sure to tell Liz how excited you were that I brought you home safely!" Roxy cooed into little Roxie's ear as she wiped the dog's paws and let her inside. "You be a good girl!"

Roxy laughed as little Roxie immediately plopped down on her purse-shaped lounge pillow. Everything little Roxie had was over the top and girly—including a hot-pink collar that spelled "ROXIE" in rhinestones.

Be @ school in a flash…just rescued L'il R! She's @ home safe & sound.

Roxy hurried off to school—as fast as she could with boots that squeezed her feet with every step. *Okay, we're off to a shaky start*, she sighed. *But this still is my year!*

DOGGY CONFESSIONAL
LITTLE ROXIE

What a strange morning! I mean, my dog walker just let me out of the house without a leash! I'll tell you, sister, she was mad about something—going on and on about how I live in such a big house but my owners are really cheap! I almost lost my biscuits when I heard that.

I bet Liz will yell at her the way she was yelling on the phone this morning. I'm not sure what was going on, but she was downright rabid. It had something to do with Roxy. When Roxy texted her this morning, Liz just shook her head and ignored it. I smell a scuffle brewing. I saw the way Liz was showing her teeth and snarling. She was ready to attack!

When it comes to Liz and Roxy, it's obvious who reigns as alpha dog.

Chapter Two

ROXY WINCED WITH EVERY step she took, but she ignored the pain because nothing mattered right now except making her grand entrance at school. Her breathing returned to normal as she finally made her way onto the Monroe Middle School grounds.

She was all set to break into a mad dash to the front steps—but she couldn't. The normally peaceful front lawn looked about as insane as the mall on the day after Thanksgiving—that is, if the mall were overrun with dogs (and a few cats for good measure).

Dogs used notebooks as Frisbees and backpacks as chew toys and annoyingly begged every student, teacher, and janitor for affection and treats. The pets all looked lost and confused—and that just irritated Roxy. She crossed her arms in a huff as she stood in the middle of the chaos, and frantically tried to spot Liz or *anyone* she knew.

Principal West stood at the front entrance. He tried to guide the dogs back outside and the students inside, but it was no use. Dark stains of sweat pooled around his armpits, and his bushy eyebrows wiggled up and down. Poor Principal West was more frazzled than ever.

"Move along, everyone!" he yelled into a megaphone

with exasperation. "I will not hesitate to give a detention to any student who's not sitting in homeroom by the last bell." After two golden retrievers ran through his legs and into the building, he finally sat down on the steps with his head in his hands.

Roxy made a mental note to ask Liz at lunch if she thought Principal West wore a toupee and then sat down on a bench to adjust her boots. At this point, she didn't care if she got detention. She was in agony and wondered if she could get into trouble for showing up to class barefoot. Roxy was about to try walking again when a mob of dogs led by Kim Pierce blocked her path.

Kim, known as the "Dog Whisperer" by the students of Monroe Middle School, cared for dogs more than anything else in the world. Dogs were her only friends, and Roxy and Liz thought she was super-weird.

"Excuse me! Watch where you're going!" Kim demanded as she tried to steer some mutts away from the dumpster. Roxy wasn't sure if Kim was talking to the dogs or to the students that almost stepped on them. "Animals can and will have panic attacks if they don't have enough space!"

Roxy wished Liz was with her to witness this. It was almost as good as the day last year in Algebra when the room suddenly began to smell like wet dog food. Nobody was certain where the stink was coming from, but when Kim walked to the chalkboard to demonstrate the solution to a tricky equation and a big open packet of smelly dog treats fell from her pocket, the class's suspicions were confirmed.

Liz and Roxy had burst out laughing. When Liz asked if Kim was wearing "Eau de Dog-ay," Roxy had thought she just might pee her pants. The rest of the class started howling and barking. Kim didn't cry—she just went back to her seat with a stone face. Now, at *least* ten dogs surrounded Kim, and, of course, she had more than enough treats for them all.

This must be like her birthday and Christmas all in one! Roxy laughed to herself as she watched Kim try to stuff a teacup poodle into her backpack. Kim stood and started walking backward, and all the dogs followed as she called out commands. With each step she took, Kim inched closer and closer to a smoldering pile of fresh poop. The words "Look out!" popped into Roxy's head, but she couldn't get them out in time. Roxy heard a "squish," and Kim Pierce was knee deep in dog poop.

"*Gross!*" a loud voice boomed, followed by several gagging sounds. "I'm totally going to throw up, Kim!"

The commotion drew a crowd. Kim, however, cared way more about the pug eating someone's Biology book than that her pink Converse sneakers were now brown and stinky. Kim left sloppy, smelly footprints as she ran over to stop the pug.

"Seriously, Kim…" The voice was loud and harsh. "Can't you smell that?"

The crowd had doubled in size, and everyone was laughing—and pinching their noses. Roxy even noticed one of the janitors trying to hold back a smirk. The voice belonged to none other than Georgia Sweeney. Roxy should've known; that girl said whatever came to her mind. It was like she had no filter in her brain to stop herself.

"It's not my fault. These dogs are off their schedules, and routine is very important for a dog's well-being," Kim said. The growing crowd laughed louder. "Dogs have sensitive digestive systems and they don't deal well with stress, so they poop…It's their way of communicating."

Hearing the word "poop" was too much for the boys to handle.

"Maybe you need a diaper!"

"Stink bomb!"

"Dog freak!"

Roxy wished she had some popcorn for this show. *Where is Liz?* Roxy knew things were out of whack today, but it wasn't like Liz to miss out on a spectacle—especially one like this. Liz had a sixth sense about when drama was unfolding.

"If you're such a dog expert, why don't you have a pooper-scooper?" Georgia asked with a gag.

Kim tried to wipe off the dog poop with a small dog-treat wrapper, but it was no use. She was flustered from all the laughter, and she was much more concerned with helping the dogs than with herself.

"I seriously have to go and puke," Georgia said as she ran toward the front entrance. "This has been the most wretched morning ever!"

The final bell rang, and everyone—including the

dogs—scattered. Roxy didn't move. She wanted to delay the pain from walking in her boots for as long as possible. Principal West was now in the faculty parking lot directing traffic so teachers could park their cars without running over any dogs. Roxy knew he was far too busy to give out detentions. Many dogs had followed their owners to school, so a lot of kids were still outside trying to command their pets to go home. Roxy texted Liz:

Where R U?!

It wasn't like Liz to go so long without texting her back. Their BlackBerries were practically attached to their hands.

"Come here, Bella. Yes, that's a good girl," Kim cooed to a fluffy, little Havanese. "Yes, if you get in my bag, I promise to take good care of you."

Roxy shook her head while Kim smuggled the dog into her book bag and threw treats at the sad-looking dogs she was leaving behind. The janitor had let Kim dip her feet into his bucket of water to get them cleaned up. Now her shoes sloshed and left small puddles with every step—but that was much better than a trail of poop.

Roxy stood, steadied herself, and took slow steps toward homeroom. She prayed she had at least one morning class with Liz. There was no way she could wait until lunch to fill her friend in on all the drama that had gone down this morning!

DOGGY CONFESSIONAL
BELLA

My, my! I do like that Kim Pierce. She knows how a pure-bred deserves to be treated.

I don't know why all of those mangy kids were laughing at her. Don't they know good manners and etiquette? They certainly are not from a genteel breed, such as the Pomeranian!

I've seen some downright untrainable pooches at the dog park, but they make these girls look tame. Before Kim scooped me off my delicate paws, this nippy group of girls started yap, yap, yapping at me for sitting on one of their "designer" purses! And then the leader of their ferocious pack said I was much more civilized than someone else they know...who doesn't have the excuse of being a dog. A girl named Roxy. She must have done something totally fierce. The pack went wild talking about it!

Chapter Three

WHERE IN THE WORLD is she? Roxy panicked as she paced anxiously by the entrance to the cafeteria. She desperately scanned the crowd looking for Liz and the rest of their friends so they could grab food and claim their picnic table for the year. Ever since Poop Gate (as it was known throughout school) had erupted that morning, Liz had stayed MIA and not returned a single one of Roxy's text messages. Dogs were popping up everywhere—from classrooms to lockers to even bathroom stalls—later in the day. Teachers didn't bother teaching. Roxy had finally given in to her aching feet and traded her chic, stylish boots for her gym sneakers. Liz would be disgusted, but Roxy feared a sprained ankle would have been in her future. Gym shoes for the day were a much cuter option than crutches for a month.

Principal West and a blockade of teachers, janitors, and a few muscular jocks stood at the cafeteria doors in a desperate attempt to keep the dogs out.

"Kids! We'll take care of the dogs—you worry about getting your lunch!" Principal West scolded the students that stopped to pet the dogs. "Move along or detention! The choice is yours!"

Roxy had no choice but to make her way to the lunch counter—alone. Liz and Roxy should have arrived together. Roxy had visualized this moment all summer long. They would link arms and claim their picnic table for the year.

I hope Liz wasn't kidnapped by one of the striking dog walkers! Roxy thought as she picked up a salad, an apple, and a celebratory "first day of school" cookie. *Maybe they're holding her as ransom for better wages.*

But when Roxy stepped outside, she immediately realized Liz was out of harm's way. Roxy couldn't believe it. Liz was already holding court at a picnic table under the big tree. She was laughing hysterically and flipping through magazines with the rest of the girls.

"Liz! I've been looking all over for you." Roxy rushed over and tried to squeeze into the spot next to Liz on the bench. "Can you believe these dog walkers? Did you get my text about rescuing little Roxie?"

Liz was petite with wavy blond hair that cascaded perfectly to the middle of her back. Her lips were so red that she didn't need lip gloss—just a dab of something clear to make them shine. Liz was always poised and in control of every situation. Her years of competing in beauty pageants made it hard sometimes to tell if she was being real or practicing one of her acts. Her bedroom was covered from wall to wall with sashes, crowns, and trophies that she had been winning since she was a little girl.

Most of Liz's weekends were consumed with traveling across the country to compete for those coveted crowns.

Liz spent a lot of time during the week prepping: she had regular spray tans, got fitted for wigs in every color and hairstyle, and took all sorts of classes—from ballet to improv—to give her a "talent" in the competitions.

Liz's deep-blue eyes were her trademark. She had won "Prettiest Eyes" at five pageants in a row. When she smiled, her eyes twinkled like stars. But when she was angry, they turned into gray, stormy little slits. Roxy had never seen them look as small and frightening as they did right now.

"I don't know *what* you did because my housekeeper Rosie found little Roxie shivering in a corner," Liz said coolly. "Not that it's any of your business, but Rosie has the afternoon off so she had no choice but to bring Roxie here. She's in my bag."

Roxy heard scuffling in Liz's hot-pink dog carrier, which most people would mistake for an oversize purse. Roxy swallowed hard. *Am I having an out-of-body experience?* she wondered.

"None of my business?" Roxy asked. She was shocked and confused. "What's going on?"

The lunch table went silent. The other girls put their heads down and pretended to check their cell phones.

"You're a liar. That's what's going on," Liz seethed. "And you'd better get up from this table because we have no room for traitors here."

"*Traitor? Liar?*" Roxy stammered. This was a nightmare. It had to be. Her alarm would ring any minute so she could wake up and start her first day of school for real. "What are you…?"

"You lied about being my best friend," Liz cut her off and stood up. Liz was a tiny girl, but she suddenly appeared larger than life. "Because my best friend would never betray me the way you did this summer."

Everyone at nearby tables stopped eating. They all stared at Liz and Roxy. The queen bees were already at each other's throats on the first day of school? It didn't get juicier than this. And Liz loved an audience, so Roxy knew this was about to get even uglier.

"Betray you?" Roxy asked quietly. "What are you talking about?

"Did you or did you not kiss Matt Billings this summer?" Liz pounded her fist on the table for dramatic effect. "When I was at pageant camp? Ring any bell?"

Roxy gulped. Roxy and Liz both worshipped the ground that Matt Billings walked on—every girl in school had a major crush on him. His brown hair was thick and just a little too long. When it fell into his eyes, he whipped it to the side with a swift flip of his head, better revealing big brown eyes rimmed with long, thick lashes.

Matt also had an irresistible smile, and the best part about it was the set of dimples that popped up every time he laughed. (Roxy also had noticed that lately his trademark T-shirts looked a little snug. The result of long hours at baseball camp, she assumed.)

Over the summer, Matt had played baseball every

afternoon in the park. Roxy and Liz had spent hours sun-bathing near his field just to catch a glimpse of his cute butt in those tight pants. They pinky-swore over the Fashion Bible that they wouldn't let a boy come between them.

So when Liz got the guts to ask Matt to hang out, Roxy tried her hardest to act happy for her friend. But then Liz had to leave town for three weeks for pageant camp, delaying her date with Matt. It wasn't Roxy's fault that she kept bumping into Matt at the park.

Everything had started so innocently. After the third time they ran into each other, Matt had suggested that they grab some frozen yogurt at the mall. Talking to him had been so easy and fun. He was such a goofball that Roxy soon started to forget she had a crush on him.

He teased her mercilessly about the too-tight shoes that Liz made her wear, or he hid her cell phone and some-times waited hours to reveal that he'd had it all along. Roxy couldn't wait for Liz to get back from camp so the three of them could hang out. How great that she got along so well with Liz's boyfriend! Right? Wrong.

On the night before Liz was due back in town, Matt unexpectedly stopped by Roxy's house.

"Hey, Loser," Roxy said with a smile when she saw him standing on her porch. His muscles glistened with sweat—something she and Liz would have spent hours daydreaming about—but now Roxy barely noticed. "I was just going to the bakery to pick up a welcome-home cupcake for Liz. You wanna come?"

"Um, sure," Matt said nervously. "I guess I should get Liz something too."

Roxy shrugged, and the two of them headed to the bakery. Roxy thought he was a little quieter than normal, but she didn't think anything of it—until they reached the counter. The bakery was deserted and no one was there to take their order. Roxy pressed her nose to the glass case to check out the cupcake options while they waited.

"Should we get Liz chocolate or vanilla frosting?" Roxy asked, and Matt answered by leaning over and kissing her.

It happened so fast that Roxy didn't know what to do except panic. The guy her best friend had claimed for herself had just kissed *her* on the lips…in public.

"This never happened, Matt!" Roxy squealed. "Liz is my best friend!"

"Roxy, come on…you can't tell me you didn't feel something this summer," Matt insisted.

"You're my *friend*, and so is Liz!" Roxy pleaded. "Please, don't tell her. You have to swear!" Roxy begged Matt to keep the kiss a secret, and after much convincing, he reluctantly swore on his baseball glove that he would never tell Liz—or anyone else.

So, who in the world told on us? Roxy wondered.

"So, is it true?" Liz demanded. "It's a simple yes-or-no question."

"Liz, you're my best friend…" Roxy stammered. She had no idea how to fix this. "It was no big deal!"

"I *knew* it," Liz said while pausing to scan the crowd that had now gathered. Matt stood off to the side with his arms crossed. He kept looking like he was going to say something and then like he'd thought better of it.

"You couldn't find a boyfriend of your own, so you had to steal mine the second I left town? Pathetic."

I can't cry…please don't let me cry in front of everyone—especially Matt!

Jessica Stevens stood by Liz's side with a smug look plastered on her face. She shot Roxy daggers with her eyes. All summer long, Liz had threatened to ban Jessica from the group because she was too needy and called Liz every five minutes. *Now she's in my spot!* Roxy wished one of the dogs would lick that smug look right off Jessica's face.

"What can I do to fix this?" Roxy pleaded. She knew she sounded desperate—and even scared. Liz was like a wolf: she smelled fear and attacked when her opponent was down. But Roxy couldn't help herself. "Can't we just put this behind us?"

Liz looked at Roxy like she had just suggested they run naked through the school yard.

"We're finished," Liz sneered. "*You're* finished."

Roxy felt paralyzed. She stood in front of the picnic table unable to move a muscle. Everyone was staring at her. Roxy could tell they felt sorry for her—and relieved they weren't in her place. Where was she going to eat lunch? No one would ever want to be friends with the girl who stole

Liz Craft's guy. Roxy's reign as queen bee was over before it had even started. She turned to walk away.

"Oh, Roxy?" Liz cooed. "Just one more—um, wait... are you wearing gym shoes in broad daylight?"

"The boots were too tight..." Roxy tried to get the words out, but she didn't even know why she bothered. Liz and all the girls at the table burst out laughing.

"It doesn't matter that you kissed Matt because I would never be seen in public with you in those shoes outside of the gym!" Liz fumed. "I mean, violating the Fashion Bible on the first day of school? Really, Roxy!"

Come on, tears...stay in. Don't make this even more humiliating for me! Roxy prayed, but it was too late. A single tear slid down her cheek. *Who is this awful girl, and what did she do with my best friend Liz?*

"I didn't violate it. I have the boots in my bag..." Roxy stammered.

"You better have the Fashion Bible in there too," Liz responded. "It doesn't belong to you anymore! Good luck getting dressed without my help. I'm sure a *skort* would look lovely with those smelly sneakers!"

Roxy heard the shrieks of laughter as she ran off. She desperately searched for a spot far, far away from Liz. Roxy still didn't want to cry, but before she knew it, a gush of tears plopped onto her ugly gym shoes like big, fat raindrops.

DOGGY CONFESSIONAL
LITTLE ROXIE

So, I don't get it. I mean, Matt clearly likes Roxy—he's allowed, right? I overheard Liz ask him when they could finally hang out so she could tell him all about pageant camp. Poor Matt must not be the brightest bulb because he asked if Roxy could come too.

When Liz started interrogating him about why he wanted Roxy there, I knew he was in trouble. As expected, Liz freaked out when he revealed that he had been hanging out with Roxy while Liz was gone. No wonder he spilled the beans about their kiss!

Chapter Four

ROXY WAS CRYING SO hard she could barely see where she was going. She wanted to run past the school gates and keep going until she was far away from Liz, Matt, the dogs, and school.

I'll just start over, dye my hair, change my name. Is there a witness-protection program for girls shunned by their popular best friends? Roxy wondered as she desperately tried to find somewhere quiet to hide for the rest of lunch.

She just wanted to find a safe spot to dry her tears and collect her thoughts. She finally collapsed under a shady tree far from the masses and pulled out a mirror to fix the blotchy makeup mess that was now all over her face. A few stray dogs came up to Roxy looking for affection, but she was in no mood.

"You dogs have ruined my day already—get out of here!" Roxy hissed. "Go on, move it!"

The dogs whimpered and tried to lick Roxy's face one last time before wandering off. Roxy felt bad, but she didn't have it in her to be nice to anyone right now—not even those confused and helpless dogs.

"You know, they just wanted you to pet their heads. Dogs are like people. They need reassurance."

Roxy was startled that anyone was talking to her. She

thought she'd picked a spot far enough away from human contact. But Kim Pierce stood a few feet from her—with the same dogs Roxy had shooed away now happily eating treats out of Kim's hands.

Great...I found my way to Dog Central Station. Roxy let out a long, deep sigh.

"Um, that's nice," she mumbled. She didn't mean to be rude, but she would much rather be alone than making small talk with Kim about dogs.

"I'm really not in the mood for any kind of company right now."

Kim sighed, pulled a small ball out of her bag, and tossed it around with the pack of dogs that surrounded her.

Roxy buried her head in her hands. How had she managed to go in one day from seventh-grade queen to such a lonely outcast that Kim Pierce was the only person paying her an ounce of attention? Roxy felt the weight of someone else's eyes on her. She looked up. Georgia Sweeney was sitting a few feet away. She lowered her gaze when she realized that Roxy had noticed her staring. Georgia just snickered to herself while knitting fast and furiously.

She knits? Like my ninety-year-old grandmother? Roxy wanted to scream. She prayed her BlackBerry would connect to the school's Wi-Fi even though she was so far from the main building. She needed to start researching boarding schools—anything to get far away from Kim, Georgia, all these dogs, and, most of all, Liz Craft. Roxy was sure her parents would understand.

I'm not going to survive a year eating lunch solo while watching Kim's Best in Show and being judged by Little Miss Knitter.

Someone tapped Roxy on her shoulder, and she nearly jumped out of her skin. Roxy hoped it was Liz. Maybe she'd realized that the scene by the picnic tables was slightly over the top and wanted to apologize. But instead, an annoying dog walker was trying to hand Roxy a flyer that explained the outlandish and ridiculous demands of their strike. Roxy started pounding the buttons on her BlackBerry. She needed to find a way to get out of town because she couldn't take much more.

"Attention, students of Monroe Middle School! This is Principal West."

A hush fell over the lawn as everyone strained to hear what Principal West had to say. The last time he'd interrupted lunch had been the previous spring. The school had closed down for an afternoon then so MTV could film a reality show in the halls.

"Due to the dog-walkers' strike, we are declaring tomorrow 'Bring Your Dog to School Day.'"

He paused while students started stomping their feet and cheering. The noise got so loud that all the dogs on campus started howling and barking in response.

"You must get a permission form from the front office. It must be signed by your parents and turned in when you and your pet arrive at school tomorrow!"

Roxy groaned. Kim clapped her hands and squealed in

delight. Georgia just kept knitting. Didn't Principal West realize that technically *today* was Bring Your Dog to School Day? Roxy wished she could find a way to get Principal West to pin the blame for all this doggy mayhem on Liz. It was no use, though. Even if Roxy could come up with a way, Liz's specialty was sucking up to adults. Liz should have had hundreds of detentions over the years, but she just batted her eyelashes and gave a "Who, me?" look that got her out of trouble every time.

Roxy looked over at Georgia knitting away. She must have stared a little too long because Georgia put her needles down and gave Roxy a nasty look.

"Can I help you?" Georgia sneered. "If you take a picture, it might last longer!"

"I, uh, I was just looking at the dogs over there," Roxy stammered.

Roxy knew that she wasn't exactly Georgia's favorite person—and the feeling was definitely mutual. One year ago to the day, on the first day of sixth grade, Roxy and Liz had met Georgia for the first time. She had just transferred to Monroe Middle School, so she was standing in the hall all alone, looking at her schedule.

With her petite figure, raven-black hair, and deep-blue eyes, Georgia looked like she belonged in their group. Unfortunately, Georgia had unknowingly picked out the same T-shirt as Liz to wear to school that morning. They both were wearing a vintage, rock 'n' roll baby tee from the legendary music club CBGB in New York City. Liz's cousin had actually worked there in the '70s, so Liz's shirt was authentic.

Of course, Georgia couldn't help but overhear Liz mocking her cheap, department-store version. Everyone in the hallway heard Liz go on and on. Anyone else in school would have just walked away and let Liz have her moment. But not Georgia Sweeney. She took one look at Liz's hair extensions and announced that Liz "looked like Barbie's cousin...totally fake!"

Georgia was officially declared "toxic." The news that everyone should stay away from the "big-mouthed new girl" spread like wildfire. Georgia had sat in the outskirts of the lunch area ever since—and always received nasty looks from Roxy and Liz whenever they crossed paths.

Now Georgia collected her things and stomped off without saying good-bye. Not that Roxy expected her to say anything—but she couldn't take much more of being ignored. The ball that Kim was tossing to the stray dogs rolled into Roxy's schoolbag.

"Um, excuse me," Kim called over meekly. "Can you throw it back? You can play with us if you want."

Roxy rolled her eyes and pushed the ball back on the ground toward Kim and her pack of dogs.

"No thanks," Roxy muttered as she started to collect her things. Kim was now surrounded by at least ten dogs. They seemed to instinctively know that Kim would take care of them.

"Cookie, play dead!" Kim commanded. A foxhound

instantly rolled over onto its back. If Roxy wasn't in such a bad mood, maybe she would have been more impressed. Instead, the scene just made her feel worse.

Standing up to leave, Roxy noticed something silver and shiny a few feet away. It was one of Georgia's knitting needles. The "devil Roxy" on one shoulder encouraged her to leave it behind (or throw it into the bushes), while the "angel Roxy" on the other shoulder told her to throw it in her bag and track down Georgia later.

Why does the angel always win? Roxy sighed as she dropped the knitting needle into her book bag and started to make her way back toward the main building. So far, Roxy and Liz weren't in any of the same classes together. Roxy hoped the same was true for her remaining afternoon classes.

DOGGY CONFESSIONAL
COOKIE

People are calling my new friend "Kim of Bark." I'd take the nickname as a compliment, but I don't think she likes it too much.

And I wasn't fooled when Liz tried to give me a note to bring to Kim.

She told me it was Roxy Davis's adoption papers. Her friends laughed when Liz explained that since Roxy was now an orphan, Kim should take her in. But Roxy is not of any canine breed I know. So I just ignored Liz and walked away. But not before I saw her snarl at me.

Just for that, I let out a little bit of gas during my departure. Liz looked at her friend Jessica, wrinkled her nose, and made a sour face. I'll never tell that it was me!

Chapter Five

THE LAST BELL FINALLY rang, and Roxy let the sea of dogs, teachers, and students push her to the front of the courtyard. Her cell phone buzzed for the first time all afternoon. Roxy felt a jolt of hope. Maybe it was Liz?

> The roads are still a mess. U need to walk home. Sorry, Pumpkin. Love, Dad

Roxy tried to fight back tears for the second time that day as she made her way to the sidewalk. With her head down, she desperately searched her bag for her iPod. Music always cheered her up. But then Roxy remembered the iPod was still docked to her alarm clock in her bedroom.

"Roxy!" a voice called out. "Roxy!"

It was Liz. Roxy breathed a sigh of relief. Liz was going to apologize. Within minutes, they would start laughing about how this was just a big misunderstanding, link arms, and join the other girls to celebrate the first day of school over frozen yogurt at the mall. Roxy knew that Liz could never stay mad at her for long.

"Hey!" Roxy said with a smile. "I'm so glad you…"

"I need the Fashion Bible," Liz said tersely. She sneered at Roxy and held her hand out expectantly. "It doesn't belong to you anymore, so if it's in your bag, hand it over."

"I don't have it," Roxy said. Her heart sank into her grungy, unfashionable gym socks. Seventh grade officially sucked. "It's at home."

"Do I hear an attitude?" Liz asked. Once again, a small crowd formed almost immediately around them. Roxy wasn't surprised. It was Liz vs. Roxy. In one corner was Liz, the most notorious queen bee in the history of Monroe Middle School. And in the other corner was Roxy, the queen bee who had recently lost her crown—along with any hope of ever having a social life. It was like a made-for-TV movie and a reality show rolled into one. And, since it *was* the first day of school, no one had anything else to gossip about except the dogs. So, for now, the crowd circled Liz and Roxy and waited for the sparring to begin.

"Maybe," Roxy muttered under her breath. Then, she spun around and stomped away—holding her head as high as she could manage while feeling totally defeated.

"Keep walking! Good thing you have on your smokin' hot sneakers!" Liz yelled after her.

Little Roxie barked in response, as if to say, "That's right! You're a failed fashionista." Roxy had a feeling that little Roxie knew better than to cross Liz—just like everyone else at school.

"You're much better without that phony girl."

Roxy looked up just in time to avoid bumping into Georgia, who seemed to appear out of nowhere.

Why can't I escape her? And why does she always look like she's sizing me up?

Roxy's first instinct was to ignore Georgia, but at this point, her day was already ruined. Besides, no one else was talking to her, so a conversation with Georgia was better than nothing. But that didn't mean Roxy planned to let Georgia slip into her life as her new BFF.

"Oh yeah?" Roxy asked. "What do you know about phony? You think you're so great—tell me, how many friends do you have?"

"Just answer this: what do you talk about besides how Liz Craft thinks she's more important than the President of the United States?" Georgia asked with a laugh. "Oh wait, let me guess—you also talk about how Liz Craft thinks no one looks better than her in clothes. Or how beautiful she looks in cubic-zirconia-encrusted pageant crowns. And what are those fake teeth called—flippers?"

Roxy felt herself start to smile. She even had to suppress a laugh. She couldn't let Georgia know that she wasn't that far off from the truth about Liz.

Yes, Liz is self-absorbed, but she was still a good friend to me. Wasn't she? Roxy wondered.

"Whatever," Roxy said quietly. "We're just having an off day. Everyone is stressed because of the dog-walkers' strike. We'll be back on track tomorrow."

Georgia let out a snort. "Wow! If you believe that, then I believe a dog is going to overthrow Principal West." She laughed. "I mean, honestly, it's not so bad eating lunch by the fence. It's quiet, and you can get a lot of homework done…"

"I'm sure things will be back to normal tomorrow," Roxy mumbled. "Liz is just having a bad day."

"If you say so," Georgia said as she turned down the street that led to her house. "You know what they say about denial…it's never in style!"

Roxy stared after Georgia. What a nosy freak! She started to walk away in a huff, but she banged into something white and fluffy, and fell forward.

"What the…?" Roxy exclaimed. An oversized sheepdog was lounging in the middle of the sidewalk and didn't so much as budge when Roxy crashed into him. "These dogs are ruining my life!"

"Sorry! I was looking all over for him!" Kim said breathlessly as she came running over with about seven other dogs trailing behind her. "You know that you really shouldn't yell around a dog that you don't know. Even a gentle dog can be set off when it senses anger…"

Roxy just let Kim keep rambling and walked on without saying a word in response. She just wanted to get home and put this day behind her. She'd discovered a website during study hall that she was anxious to look over in more depth at home. It was for a student-exchange program in Australia. Unless she joined a shuttle mission to the moon,

Australia was about as far away from Monroe Middle School as she could get.

Roxy finally made it home and quietly unlocked the door. She slowly let it shut without a sound and caught a whiff of dinner baking in the oven. Her mom was making a macaroni-and-cheese casserole with a special ingredient—sliced hot dogs.

It was Roxy's favorite dinner even though everyone, including her parents, thought it was disgusting. Her mom only made it on the first day of school and on Roxy's birthday. Right now, Roxy didn't have the heart to tell her mom that her appetite was gone. She managed to make it up to her bedroom before anyone noticed.

Now what? Roxy wondered? *Liz and I should be texting like crazy or hanging at the mall.*

Roxy flopped down on her bed and opened her laptop. Her Twitter feed popped up, and as Roxy scanned the list, she instantly was made sick to her stomach by what she read.

@TIARALIZ: My girls, the mall, and that hot server @ Yogurt Station. Happy 1st day of school 2 us!

Girls? Yogurt Station? Hot server? Without me? Roxy felt a too-familiar knot in her stomach and tried to hold back a flood of tears. She felt like the loneliest girl to ever walk the halls of Monroe Middle School. Without her friends, who was she?

"Roxy? Can I come in?"

Somehow Roxy's mom had figured out that her daughter was home and had been lurking on the other side of the bedroom door. If she stayed really quiet, Roxy wondered, would her mom think a dog on the loose had kidnapped her? Maybe that would give her a few more minutes of peace. She wanted to avoid telling her mom about her humiliating day.

"I'm kind of busy," Roxy lied. "Can we talk later?"

Her mom opened the door anyway and sat down next to her on the bed.

"I heard about all those dog walkers going on strike! What an exciting day!" she said. "Good thing we don't have a dog, huh?"

Roxy shrugged her shoulders.

"I hear that you can bring your dog to school tomorrow," her mom said with a chuckle. "Are you going to help Liz with little Roxie?"

Roxy wasn't sure what to say. Why were moms so nosy? She just wanted to be left alone.

"I don't know, Mom. I haven't talked to her about it yet," Roxy said as she played with the bottom of her ugly gym sneaker. "I want to get started on my homework…"

Her mom stood up to leave.

"Are you sure you're okay?" she asked. "You don't sound very excited. Especially with the way you've been carrying on about starting the seventh grade all summer long."

"I'm fine. I'm just tired. Is that a crime?" Roxy asked weakly.

Her mom winced and then gave her a small smile.

"Okay, okay. I get the hint," her mom said as she started to walk out of the room. But she stopped and turned back around. "Oh, do you want to invite Liz to dinner? I know she hates the hot-dog-and-macaroni casserole, but maybe little Roxie will want the leftovers."

Her mom laughed and shut the door.

Roxy was too upset to even yell something back to her mom about being rude. She stared at her cell phone. "Zero text messages" blinked back at her, and her stomach tightened once again. She had gotten used to her daily texts and phone calls with Matt. Now she couldn't even call him. Roxy had lost all her friends on just the first day of school.

She opened her laptop and went to her Facebook page. She hoped that maybe Liz had written on her wall or poked her—just something to let her know this was a major misunderstanding. But as Roxy scrolled through all her friends' status updates, she thought it was weird that she didn't see even one from Liz's account.

Liz changed her status at least three times a day because she loved telling the world everything that happened in her life. She practically tweeted on stage during her pageants, and she definitely tweeted backstage! Roxy buried her head in her hands.

Please, please, please don't let this mean what I think it does!

Roxy opened up her friend list and searched for the name "Liz Craft." Nothing came up. Roxy typed "Liz

Craft" in the search field. Liz's picture popped up with the question Roxy feared more than discovering that vampires really did exist.

Would you like to add this person as your friend?

The room started spinning, and Roxy felt like she was going to pass out.

Liz defriended me on Facebook! Already? Didn't she want to at least try to think this through? Try friend therapy? Anything?

With one click of the mouse, Liz had made it as clear as a top coat of nail polish that she and Roxy were finished—for good. Roxy was about to log off from Facebook when she noticed the list of "Friend Suggestions" up in the corner of the home page. One of them was Georgia Sweeney.

Okay, why can't I escape this girl today? Maybe it's a sign. Roxy tried to think it through rationally. *Liz defriended me. Maybe she'll come around...maybe she won't. In the meantime, I need to make some new, temporary friends.*

Roxy remembered that Georgia's knitting needle was still in her bag.

An excuse!

Without thinking, Roxy opened the phone book, scrolled her finger down the page until she located the Sweeney listing on Mulberry Drive, and dialed. The phone started ringing. There was no turning back now.

"Hello?" Georgia answered slowly and suspiciously.

"Hello, Georgia? Hi, this is Roxy Davis…" Roxy said

like she was calling Georgia on official business—and it sort of *was* business.

"Um, hey—what's up?" Georgia asked warily.

"You left behind one of your knitting needles at lunch today," Roxy said matter-of-factly. "I wanted to let you know that I have it and will bring it back to you tomorrow."

"Oh…well, thanks." Georgia was so taken off guard that she sounded genuinely grateful. "I didn't even realize it was gone."

"Yeah, I could give it back to you at lunch, but I think my dad and I pass your house on the way to school." Roxy tried to stay cool. "Would you like a ride tomorrow?"

There was a long pause. *Did she hang up on me?* Roxy wondered.

"Um, well, I usually walk and I have a dog that will be coming along, so I'm really not sure if I need a ride…"

"You have a dog?"

"Yes. Why do you sound so surprised?"

"You just never mentioned it…"

"And considering that you've spoken to the lunch lady more times than you've even looked me in the eye, why *would* you know that I had a dog?"

Georgia's venomous tongue stung Roxy through the phone, but she refused to let it get to her.

Okay, so it's no secret that she speaks her mind. Maybe that's a good quality? Just ignore it, Roxy, just ignore it. You don't have many other options right now.

"I just meant that you didn't mention it today with all

the strike stuff going on." Roxy tried to stay calm. "Do you want a ride or not? As long as your dog is in a carrier, I doubt my dad will care."

"Sure, why not?" Georgia responded. "It beats walking, and today has been strange enough. Nothing surprises me anymore."

"Great. We'll see you at 8 a.m. sharp." Roxy prayed her dad would actually be okay with making an extra stop.

"Okay. See you in the morning."

Georgia didn't even wait for Roxy to say good-bye before hanging up.

Roxy absentmindedly kept the phone to her ear and barely realized she was listening to the dial tone. She'd thought that she would feel better having some sort of social contact, but she actually felt worse.

Great—what will Liz say when she sees me arrive at school with Georgia in tow?

Roxy checked Facebook one last time to double-check that the defriending wasn't a mistake. It wasn't. Roxy noticed that all the other girls from her crew weren't showing up on her friend list anymore either.

Okay, so I'm blackballed. How many actresses fall off the radar but then land a big blockbuster movie and get back on the A-list?

She sighed. The smell from the kitchen was too hard to resist. Since something had to go right today, Roxy headed downstairs to dig into some macaroni-and-cheese-and-hot-dog casserole.

DOGGY CONFESSIONAL
LITTLE ROXIE

I'm not so sure about Liz's new pack—I smell trouble, and it does not smell pretty!

I just overheard the girls say something about Roxy being sent to eat lunch in Loserville. Is that the next town over?

They were squealing about how Matt and Roxy deserved each other. And that Liz was going to teach them a lesson.

What do they need to learn?

Chapter Six

"DOG WALKERS ON STRIKE!"
"Dog walkers need more pay!"
"Dog walkers have rights!"

Roxy pulled a pillow on top of her head and screamed. She didn't care if anyone in her house—or next door—could hear her. The striking dog walkers had been ranting since dawn right in front of her bedroom window.

The entire neighborhood was a disaster area, the dogs having destroyed the landscaping and lawns of every house on the block. But the dog walkers didn't care. They were almost proud of the damage and kept protesting about how little they got paid.

Screaming was a much-needed release for Roxy. She hadn't received one text from Liz since the previous morning. She couldn't decide what to wear because she was banned from following the Fashion Bible, and her company in the car this morning was going to be Georgia Sweeney. It was like she had been zapped into an alternate universe.

Roxy gulped. This was going to be another long day.

"Roxy! We need to leave in ten minutes if you want to have time to pick up your new friend," her dad called out. "I need to get to work early."

Friend. Roxy scoffed to herself. *I wouldn't exactly call Georgia my friend. She's more like a temporary solution.*

Roxy flung her closet doors open and realized she did not have one thing in her closet that wasn't already planned out in the Fashion Bible. Liz had made Roxy clean out her closet a few weeks earlier so they could start the school year fresh. Roxy had donated at least two garbage bags filled with perfectly good outfits from last year to the local consignment shop—and now she wished she could get them back.

Would it be weird if I went to the charity store and bought back all the clothes that I had donated? Roxy wondered.

She had placed the Fashion Bible next to her book bag before she went to bed the night before. She didn't want to forget it—even though returning it to Liz went against her better judgment. Roxy wasn't sure which would be more humiliating—handing the book over or having to come up with an excuse why it was still at home. Either way she was doomed. Roxy flipped through the Fashion Bible and looked at the outfit they had planned for her tomorrow. Pink leggings, white T-shirt with a wide black belt, and sandals.

Oh, well. What will Liz do to me if I wear tomorrow's outfit today?

Roxy threw on the outfit, smeared on a little bit of lip gloss, ran a brush through her hair, and jolted out to the car to meet her dad. He took some back roads to avoid the strike, and within minutes, they pulled up in front of Georgia's two-story, bright yellow house.

Georgia was sitting on the front steps with a sparkly white dog carrier on her lap. A skinny, little tan "hot dog" was running around on the grass next to her while she held onto a rhinestone-studded leash. Roxy's dad turned around from the front seat and shot Roxy a nasty look.

"She has a dog? I don't want that dog to ruin my leather seats," he said sternly. "It'll cost a fortune to replace them."

"Oh, yeah, Dad. I guess I should have told you. She has a dog," Roxy mumbled. "I'm sorry…I forgot."

Georgia placed her dog in the carrier and took slow, hesitant steps toward the car. Roxy had never seen her look nervous before. But the second Georgia opened the car door, the nerves were gone.

"You're late," Georgia announced as she got herself situated and fastened her seat belt. Roxy heard her dad chuckle from the front seat.

"I'm sorry. I had to pick my outfit because…" Roxy trailed off. She didn't want to hear more from Georgia about why she thought Liz was such a bad person and terrible friend.

"Because now you have to think for yourself instead of doing whatever Liz tells you?" Georgia asked with a knowing look. "You're not really handing her back that wretched clothes book today, are you?"

"I, well, I'm actually wearing an outfit scheduled for tomorrow, so…"

"So that should teach them a lesson, right?" Georgia asked smugly.

Roxy was seething. She knew that Georgia was right.

I don't care. It doesn't matter because it's none of her business. No wonder she doesn't have any friends!

"No, but I do think for myself," Roxy said curtly while staring out the window. She held her breath as she watched a parade of kids walk by the car, each with their book bags in one hand and a dog leash in the other. She scanned the group looking for Liz. Roxy knew that Liz would sooner stay home than walk to school. Her housekeeper drove Liz just one block to drop her off every morning even though Liz had less than a three-minute walk to the school. But, with all the commotion this week, nothing would surprise Roxy.

"So, what's your dog's name?" Roxy asked Georgia, desperate to change the subject from Liz.

"Dixie—my grandparents are from the South, so we spend the summers in Savannah, Georgia. That's how I got my name too," Georgia said as she took out her knitting bag and started click-clacking away. Her hands were moving so fast that it looked to Roxy like someone had hit a fast-forward button.

Roxy took Georgia's knitting needle from her bag and placed it on Georgia's bag. "Wow, you're really fast!" Roxy marveled. "What are you making?"

"A sweater for Dixie," Georgia said with a smile. "I like to make sure that she's the best dressed at the dog park!"

The sweater was so cute that Roxy couldn't believe it was for a dog. It was white with a big argyle heart on the back. Roxy would definitely buy something like it at the mall if it came in a human size!

Why don't more dogs in town wear cute sweaters when it's cold? I'm sure little Roxie would love it…well, I'm sure there are tons of other dogs with owners just as fashionable as Liz that would die for cute outfits to put on their dogs.

The wheels in Roxy's head starting turning. People would definitely buy these sweaters. This could be huge. They could be the next Marc Jacobs or Juicy Couture—but for dogs! Canine couture—why didn't anyone else come up with this? Georgia could be the designer and Roxy the brains behind the operation.

"How long does it take you to knit a dog sweater?" Roxy asked casually. She would need to find just the right time to bring up the subject of a canine-couture business. For now, knowledge was power.

"Um, I don't know…like a few hours?" Georgia said as she started to put her things away. They were approaching the school. "Over the summer, I was making like three a day."

Roxy was so busy talking to Georgia and plotting this big, new business idea in her mind that she totally forgot to tell her dad that she wanted him to drop them off behind the school. She didn't want to risk Liz seeing her and Georgia together, but it was too late. The car pulled up almost directly in front of Liz, little Roxie, Jessica, Matt and his dog (a beagle named Banjo), and the rest of the crew. Roxy tried to stay cool and hoped that they wouldn't see her, but her dad was waving like a madman at Liz.

"I can't believe we haven't seen Liz yet this week!" Roxy's dad exclaimed as Liz waved back, flashing the infamous stage smile that she had learned at pageant camp. "She missed out on macaroni, cheese, and hot-dog casserole last night!"

"Hot dog with mac and cheese?" Georgia gagged. "Sounds like something a homeless person would eat."

"Don't knock it until you've tried it," Roxy said as she got out of the car and silently prayed that she could walk into the building without a scene from Liz.

Dear God, I'll stop watching bad reality TV shows and wear my retainer every night if I can just get to homeroom peacefully. Roxy took a deep breath and noticed that Georgia was watching her expectantly.

"Hey, do you want to have lunch today?" Roxy asked. She'd try to bring up their possible business venture then. "Same spot as yesterday?"

"Uh, sure," Georgia said and waved at Roxy's dad. "Thanks for the ride, Mr. Davis."

Roxy tried to ignore the stares and snickers coming from Liz and the gang as Georgia got out of the car and her dad pulled away. Roxy wanted to run after him and jump back into the backseat. Everyone seemed to have a dog with them, either on a leash or in a dog carrier. Principal West and a group of teachers stood out front collecting permission slips and handing every dog owner some dog treats and a bag to pick up poop.

"Wow!" Liz called. "Are you kidding me? Really, Roxy…"

Roxy tried to avoid eye contact with everyone in Liz's

group and practically hurdled over a poodle to get past Liz. She didn't even say good-bye to Georgia.

"I thought those gym sneakers were a lame accessory—but Georgia? You've outdone yourself!"

Roxy just kept speed walking and refused to turn around *or* cry. She felt a gust of wind rush by her, and something dropped onto the folder she was carrying.

Matt Billings and his dog swooped past her. Matt looked over his shoulder and gave Roxy a nod. She realized then that there was a folded scrap of paper on her folder with her name written in small, neat capital letters. Roxy recognized Matt's handwriting from the journals he'd shown her when they were hanging out. Everyone assumed that Matt was a "dumb jock," but he was actually a talented writer.

She looked around to see if Liz or anyone was nearby watching, but they had turned their attention to making little Roxie behave while they put pink bows over her ears.

HEY, ROXY:

I'M REALLY SORRY ABOUT ALL THIS. I'M TRYING TO FIX IT. LIZ FORCED IT OUT OF ME THAT WE KISSED. I DIDN'T WANT TO TELL HER. I'LL TALK TO YOU WHEN I CAN. HANG IN THERE.

MATT

Roxy couldn't help but smile. She knew better than anyone that betraying Liz was the worst thing in the world. But could she trust Matt? Even he couldn't go through with telling Liz no. No one could. Roxy was so hurt, though, because she really had thought that Matt was her friend—and look at the damage he'd caused.

The rest of the morning flew by. Roxy didn't see Liz or Matt again, but she was completely over Bring Your Dog to School Day. Dogs used folders and notebooks as make-shift Frisbees in the halls. They were on leashes, popping their heads out of carriers, barking at the teachers, and wrestling with one another. Roxy was relieved to finally get to lunch.

After sitting for a few minutes, Roxy anxiously looked around for Georgia and hoped she wasn't getting stood up. But before long, Dixie came bounding around the corner—dragging Georgia with her. Dixie stopped to sniff the butt of every dog they passed along the way.

Why are dogs so weird? Roxy thought to herself as a weary Georgia and a hyper Dixie finally plopped down next to her.

"Can you believe all this commotion?" Georgia asked breathlessly. She was sweating so much that Roxy wanted to hand her a stick of deodorant.

If I were sweating this much, Liz would totally start spritzing me with perfume.

Roxy just nodded in agreement.

"I mean, why didn't they just cancel school?" Georgia

asked as she poured some bottled water into a little plastic dish. Dixie greedily lapped it up.

"This was definitely not one of Principal West's smartest ideas," Roxy said. "I hope that he'll make all the dogs stay home tomorrow. This is just way too crazy."

"Hopefully, the dog walkers will be back to work by then!" Georgia said as she took her knitting supplies out of her bag. Roxy couldn't believe that Georgia was forming a tiny sweater right before her eyes.

"Hey, have you ever knitted people sweaters?" Roxy asked.

"Why? You want one?" Georgia laughed. "I know you're petite and all, but I don't think you could get this over your head."

"Well, they're super-cute. You should think about making matching sweaters for dogs and their owners," Roxy said. "I'm telling you—I bet that a lot of other doggie owners would want their dogs to look just as stylish as little Dixie!"

Roxy paused to see if Georgia looked interested. She couldn't get a read, so she kept going.

"Have you ever thought about selling these sweaters and making money?" Roxy asked. "I was thinking about it in the car this morning. We could have fashion shows and make a website and customize orders…"

"*We?*" Georgia picked up Dixie and put her in her carrier. "Did I enter the Twilight Zone here? From where I'm sitting, I'm the one knitting the sweaters. Now you want to be in business with me? Is that what you're trying to say?"

"Well, don't act so surprised. I'm a very good businesswoman. I've picked up some tips from my dad, and I know I could help you," Roxy said in her most convincing voice. She looked over and saw Kim Pierce just a few feet away with at least five dogs sitting happily in her lap. Kim cooed in the dogs' ears and fed them treats from her pocket.

"Maybe we could get Kim to be our consultant." Roxy couldn't believe that the words were coming out of her mouth, but she kept going. "Look at her over there! She's like a dog magnet. She literally speaks dog. I think she may even *be* part dog!"

"I don't know. I don't think Kim likes me very much, and she's sort of…uh, odd. Besides, I don't think people will want to buy my sweaters," Georgia said nervously. "Do you really think people would pay money for them?"

"I do, Georgia. I really do," Roxy said sincerely. "Let's see what Kim says. I think we need the opinion of a true dog expert!"

Roxy looked over at Kim and the gaggle of dogs lounging by her feet. Roxy's mom always told her that everyone had "something" that made them unique. Well, dogs were definitely Kim's "something"!

"Hey, Kim!" Roxy called cheerfully. "Hey! Why don't you join us over here?"

Kim looked around and seemed confused as she tried to figure out who was calling her name.

"Yoo-hoo, Kim!" Roxy frantically waved and desperately

tried to get Kim's attention. "Come over here! Join us. Bring the puppies!"

Kim rounded up the dogs and made her way over. But as soon as she sat down, Roxy and Georgia were overwhelmed by the smell of beef jerky reeking from her clothes.

"Think you may have overdone it with the treats, Kim?" Georgia blurted out with her nose wrinkled in disgust.

Roxy tried her hardest to suppress her laughter. She knew that she was going to have to be the leader in this group—and that meant not making anyone feel bad about herself.

"I have a lot of dogs to care for, if you haven't noticed. No one knows the right way to handle dogs so I'm helping out," Kim said quietly. She fed a treat to a Labradoodle named Max. "They need positive reinforcement, or they're never gonna behave."

"The dog-walkers' strike really has you stressed out, huh?" Roxy asked. She was genuinely impressed by the way Kim took care of every dog that found its way to her. She had a certain...well, power over them.

"It's not good for all these dogs to roam around the school and be so far off their normal schedules," Kim sighed as she handed two Chihuahuas a rope to wrestle over. "Why didn't Principal West ask everyone to bring proof that their dog was properly vaccinated? Or trained? And none of these dogs are getting properly hydrated."

Roxy and Georgia exchanged a look. Kim took dogs way more seriously than either of them had realized. Roxy decided that it was now or never to include her in this idea.

"Well, we actually have a dog-related idea and wanted your input," Roxy said. "No one knows more about dogs—and what dog owners want—than you do, right?"

"Right now, I think that dog owners just want their dog walkers and dog sitters back, don't you think?" Kim said as she tried to get a Shih Tzu named Jazzy to sit. "I mean, who's going to walk all these dogs? Retrain them after all these days in chaos? Make sure they're being properly fed and groomed?"

Roxy realized that Kim was absolutely right. Why stop at sweaters when they could create an entire doggie empire with dog walking, grooming, training, and, of course, a fashion line!

She felt like she was on a mission, and there was no stopping her now that her brain was spinning with ideas.

"Girls, I think we have some business to discuss," Roxy said importantly. "Overnight, this school has been turned into a two-story dog park. The neighborhood is topsy-turvy. We need our dog walkers back, but until they return, something needs to be done."

Kim and Georgia looked at Roxy like she was speaking Chinese. Even Roxy was surprised that she suddenly sounded like a mini-Donald Trump in ballet flats, but she continued her speech.

"I say we join forces and start our own dog-walking business—and add some creative extras that those striking dog walkers never even considered!"

"I thought you wanted to sell my doggy sweaters..." Georgia sounded confused. "We go to school. When would we have time to walk dogs and pull off—oh, how did you say it—creative extras?"

"Before school, after school—maybe we could get special permission to leave during lunch." Roxy was determined. Now that she had her mind set on this business, there was no turning back. "We can figure this out!"

She looked up and saw Jessica glaring at them from a distance. *Great—just what I need. Liz's little spy running back to tell her that I'm now the president of the Monroe Middle School Reject Society.*

Roxy took a deep breath and tried a different approach.

"Look, we all bring something to the table that can make this work," Roxy said earnestly. "Georgia, you can take care of doggie fashion and grooming. Kim, you can handle training, discipline, and dog whispering. And I'll do the scheduling and public relations. We'll all split the dog walking."

She looked at them and waited. The look on Georgia's face was skeptical, but she always looked at Roxy—and everyone, for that matter—like they were crazy. Kim just sat there quietly.

"Kim, you're not saying much," Georgia said. "As the so-called dog expert, what do you think about this?"

"Well, I think it's the best idea I've ever heard in my life. I want to open my own school for dogs one day, so this could be really great training." Kim paused and looked right at Roxy. "But why me? I mean, Roxy, do you really want to hang out with me?"

Roxy had known that the girls would doubt her intentions. The knot in her stomach was growing—especially with Jessica the Spy watching the entire exchange. Roxy really didn't expect Kim and Georgia to believe she was suddenly their friend, but something in her gut told her that this could work.

"I do, Kim, I really do," Roxy said, trying to not get distracted by the fact that Jessica was actually taking notes. "We're on the verge of something huge here, girls! Are you in, or are you out?"

Georgia and Kim glanced over at each other. Roxy could tell that they were skeptical, but they didn't have anything to lose—unlike Roxy.

"Well, I have about five sweaters already done that we can put up for sale right away," Georgia said as she pulled the sweater she was currently knitting from her bag. "And this one is almost finished, so I could start working on new ones after school."

"I'm in too," Kim said as she picked up the Chihuahuas, which were using Roxy's bag as a bed. "We need to make sure that one of our services is diet planning. So many dogs don't get enough of their proper nutrients because owners think that canned dog food is good enough…" Kim stopped mid-sentence when she realized that Roxy and Georgia were staring at her like she had four legs and a tail herself.

"I'm sorry. I just know a lot about dogs," Kim said sheepishly. "Isn't that why you want me here?"

"As long as you don't bore us to death," Georgia muttered.

"Okay, we have a lot of work to do," Roxy said in

her most professional voice. "We need a name, logo, flyers, list of services, website, business cards, price guide, T-shirts, supplies…"

She stopped talking because she felt a tap on her shoulder. Jessica was towering over her with arms crossed and lips pursed into a tight little smirk. Roxy gulped so hard she thought she might choke. Kim and Georgia looked a little paler than usual too.

"Hello, Roxy," Jessica sneered. "I don't mean to interrupt this, uh, meeting, is it? But I believe that you have something that doesn't belong to you."

Roxy wanted the grass she was sitting on to swallow her whole. With all of the might she could muster, she reached into her bag and pulled out the Fashion Bible.

"Is this what you're looking for?" Roxy asked.

"It's only Liz's now," Jessica said triumphantly. "I hope you don't have too much trouble getting dressed in the morning. Though dogs don't know a tube top from tube socks, so you'll be fine on your walks."

Roxy knew it—Jessica *had* been eavesdropping on their entire conversation.

"It's none of your business what I wear or what I do," Roxy said under her breath. "You can't even dress yourself without Liz's permission."

"Good luck getting this dog-walking business off the ground," Jessica laughed. "Especially with these two mutts as your business partners."

Roxy sat there paralyzed. She couldn't move or speak.

Kim suddenly pointed to the Fashion Bible and blurted out, "Treat!" Kim's dog, a Maltese named Izzy, leapt from her lap and made a mad dash for the book. In one swift motion, Izzy leapt into the air and grabbed the Fashion Bible out of Jessica's grip.

The four girls watched in shock as Izzy ran off with the book in her mouth and the Chihuahuas at her heels. Within seconds, the book was a pile of doggie drool and scraps... and completely ruined. Pages of notes and pictures—a full summer of painfully scrutinized work—were now literally blowing away in the wind.

"You *will* pay for this!" Jessica cried. She tried to salvage what was left of the spiral notebook, but it was too slobber-soaked and mangled to repair. "Just wait until I tell Liz!"

Jessica stormed back to the picnic table. Roxy and Georgia stared at Kim in disbelief.

"Kim," Roxy stammered. "Thank you."

"Wow," Georgia said. "I didn't know you had it in you. Do you have a death wish?"

"No, of course not," Kim blushed. "I don't know... it just seemed like the right thing to do. They're mean to me all the time. So, what were you saying about going into business?"

Roxy ignored the knot in her stomach and her growing anxiety about how Liz might seek revenge. If Kim didn't care, then Roxy wasn't going to let it get her down either.

"Okay, so my dad is a hard-core businessman, and I've always been told I have a sixth sense for it too," Roxy said with the confidence in her tone returning. "I sold the most Girl Scout cookies in my troop six years in a row, and my lemonade stands were always the biggest and brightest on the block. So, I think with all our talents we can really do something big. Are you guys in, or are you out?"

"I swear," Georgia said as she placed her hand on top of the sweater she was knitting and held it to her chest. "I swear on this doggie sweater that I'm in."

"Me too," Kim said as she put her hand on top of a bag of dog treats and placed it over her chest. "I swear on these Doggie Doodles!"

At that moment, Roxy felt the weight of eyes drilling a hole into her back. She looked up and saw that Jessica had dragged Liz to a few feet away and was pointing over at them. Roxy's heart dropped to her toes when she realized that Matt was standing with them too.

"Hey, Captain Canines!" Liz called out. "Nice going with the Fashion Bible. I can't wait to tell Principal West that you destroyed my personal property. You won't be walking any dogs from detention."

Kim and Georgia exchanged nervous looks, but Roxy just pretended that Liz was one of the crazy ladies on the crosstown bus who talked to themselves. Roxy's mom always told her it was better to ignore them. They would stop if they realized they weren't getting any attention, she said. Roxy hoped her mom was right!

"Okay, then our first planning meeting is immediately

after school at my house," Roxy said. "Bring a notebook and lots of ideas—we have a lot of work to do, girls!"

"Can we bring our dogs?" Kim asked. "I have to at least bring Izzy …maybe the Chihuahuas too."

"I think my mom will only be cool with one dog each." Roxy tried not to sound annoyed. She didn't have a dog of her own for a reason—her parents weren't exactly animal lovers. "Is that okay? I mean you can tie the others up out back if you *really* need to bring them."

"Tie them up? Okay, Lesson One about dog care is they do not like to be tied up." Kim put her hands on her hips. "Even domesticated, dogs are wild animals deep down and need to roam free…"

"Okay, okay, Kim. We get it," Georgia snapped. "Can you bring just one dog, or is it going to be a problem?"

"I'll bring one dog," Kim mumbled as she wrestled away leftover chunks of paper from the Fashion Bible that Izzy was still gnawing on.

"Okay, so I'll see you girls at my house after school," Roxy said firmly. "Don't be late. We have way too much to do!"

The bell rang, so Georgia, Kim, and their dogs scattered in different directions. Roxy stayed for an extra minute to jot down some notes and ideas. She was about to head to English class when she saw Matt standing nearby. Luckily, he was by himself.

"Let me guess…Liz had something to do with that note you gave me?" Roxy asked. "You know, I wasn't in this alone. I thought we *both* agreed to keep our kiss from Liz. I thought we were friends. I thought you didn't want to date Liz after all."

"I know. I'm sorry," Matt said. He sounded sincere, but Roxy didn't know who to believe nor who she could trust anymore.

"I didn't want this to happen. Liz had nothing to do with the note. I tried to tell her not to be mad at you. I swear," Matt said. "I told her not to blame you and that it was all me, but she threatened to tell Coach that I cheated on the math placement exam—even though I didn't. I could be placed on academic probation and get kicked off the team. I gotta go. Let's talk soon."

Roxy wondered if she could trust him as she watched him head toward the gym.

As she stood there trying to understand the mysterious relationship between Liz and Matt, she saw him turn and look back at her and smile. It happened lightning fast. When she blinked, Matt was gone. All Roxy knew for sure was that she was more confused than ever.

DOGGY CONFESSIONAL
BANJO

Oh, yeah! Matt and I are hotter than ever this year. We've got the females eating right out of our hands...well, at least I do. Poor Matt tries with the ladies, but he doesn't have the same touch I do.

It's totally obvious that Matt likes Roxy—the person, not the dog. I caught him looking at her Facebook pictures on his computer last night. He wrote her about a dozen texts and then deleted all of them before he hit "Send."

Matt's a good kid and he loves playing sports—but he's got no game with the ladies!

Chapter Seven

ROXY RACED HOME AFTER school to straighten up her room and warn her mother that she had some friends coming over. She tried to be as vague as possible because she wasn't quite ready to explain how and why she was going into the dog-walking business. Of course, her mom had a thousand questions anyway.

"What about Liz?" her mom asked. "Where has she been?"

Roxy glared at her mom while throwing a mound of clothes into her closet. Roxy was relieved that the Fashion Bible had been destroyed. She couldn't swallow the thought of showing up at school in the same outfit as Jessica and Liz every day for the rest of the school year.

"Mom, I can have other friends too, right?" Roxy snapped. Her mom raised an eyebrow but still agreed to bring iced tea and granola bars up to Roxy's room when the girls arrived.

During study hall, Roxy had handwritten agendas in bright pink (her signature color) and loopy, cursive handwriting. She placed three neatly stacked copies on her bed for the girls to look over during the meeting.

Dog Walkers Inc.

Meeting One Agenda
- 🐾 *Vote on company name.*
- 🐾 *Meeting dates and times.*
- 🐾 *List of services. Prices. Responsibilities.*
- 🐾 *Officially open for business!*

There was a knock on Roxy's bedroom door, and Izzy burst in with Kim right behind her. Kim carried two shopping bags that were overflowing with doggie toys, supplies, treats, and beds.

"What's all this?" Roxy asked as Izzy hopped up onto her bed in a single leap. "Are you moving in?"

"They're our supplies!" Kim explained. "My mom always yells at me for having too much dog stuff all over my room, so I'm happy to donate it all."

Kim set her backpack down on Roxy's bed, and Jazzy wriggled out.

"I'm sorry," Kim said sheepishly. "I know that you said I could only bring one dog, but I couldn't find Jazzy's owner after school and I didn't know what else to do. I promise she'll be quiet."

Jazzy squeezed herself into the slightly ajar bottom drawer of Roxy's dresser and burrowed deep inside a stack of pajama bottoms and old T-shirts.

Roxy hoped her mom wouldn't notice the stench of dog food and treats wafting from under the bedroom door. She hoped she wouldn't gag from it herself. She was about to suggest that maybe Kim could leave some of her supplies on the front porch when Georgia barged into the bedroom without knocking. She immediately zeroed in on Jazzy and Izzy's presence.

"Geez, Kim, good thing I dropped off Dixie at home since Roxy specifically said we could only bring one dog each," Georgia scoffed as she grabbed an agenda off the bed and plopped into a white rocking chair that Roxy had had since she was a baby. Georgia crossed her legs and started to look over the agenda.

"Wow, Roxy, you're really a type A personality."

Roxy took a deep breath. Was it too much to ask that Kim wouldn't be weird and Georgia wouldn't be too obnoxious?

Maybe this wasn't the greatest idea, Roxy thought to herself as she cleared her throat.

"Okay, girls, I officially call this meeting to order," she said in her most official voice as she grabbed her copy of the agenda out of Izzy's mouth and banged a hairbrush like a gavel. "I think we have what my dad would call a million-dollar idea, and we need to get started right away. Welcome to Dog Walkers Inc.!"

"Um, Dog Walkers Inc.? When did we decide on that?" Georgia asked. "I'm not sure I like it."

"That's just what I'm calling it until we decide on a name. Read the first item on the agenda—vote on a name!" Roxy sighed. "So, what do you guys think? How about the Dog Walkettes?"

"Lame," Georgia said.

"Eh," Kim said. "We're going to do more than just walk dogs, right?

"Well, what do you guys propose?" Roxy asked. "We need something catchy. Something memorable. Something we can put on flyers around town!"

"What about Barkalicious? Or Posh Pets? Or Three Girls, a Dog, and a Leash?" Georgia gave them an expectant look. She obviously thought her ideas were award winning.

"Three Girls, a Dog, and a Leash? That's way too long! We need to fit the name on a flyer and say it when we answer the phone without it being a tongue twister," Roxy pointed out. "Barkalicious could be good! Wait! I've got it! What about Walk This Way?"

"Like that Aerosmith song?" Georgia said curtly. "Uh, no. We can't name the company after an old band that my parents rock out to on the classic rock station."

"Okay, do you have a better idea?" Roxy asked. "We still have five more items to vote on!"

"Yes," Georgia said. "I do. I want to know what Kim thinks. You're awfully quiet over there."

Roxy and Georgia stared at Kim. She was rubbing Izzy's stomach and whispering softly in her ear. Finally Kim raised her head.

"Um, well…how about the Doggy Divas?" she asked hesitantly. "That's easy to say on the phone, right?"

"I love it!" Roxy clapped her hands together in excitement. "It's perfect!"

"Yeah, it's pretty cool." Georgia jumped up and wrote the name in big block letters on a dry-erase board hanging over Roxy's desk.

"All in favor say 'Aye,'" Roxy said in an official voice. The girls all sang back "Aye" in unison.

Kim sat there blushing with pride. "Thanks, guys," she said quietly.

"Yes, yes, but we have to move on! Next order of business," Roxy directed. "We need to figure out our meeting dates and times."

"How about we rotate houses? We could meet three days a week and at a different one of our houses each time," Kim asked. Roxy couldn't help but notice how much more confident Kim sounded now that they liked her business name. "We can also give out our cell phone numbers so people can text us with questions and to confirm appointments."

"Great," said Roxy as Georgia nodded in agreement. "How about we meet after school every day this week to get things going and then every Monday, Wednesday, and Friday starting next week to take appointments and discuss business?"

Georgia and Kim couldn't see any reason why not, and the motion passed unanimously. The girls decided they would charge $10 for each 30-minute walk and an additional $10 for each add-on service, such as a grooming or training session. Georgia's sweaters would sell for $20 each, including a free doggy fashion consultation.

"Okay, girls, gather around the computer!" Roxy was

exhausted. The afternoon had been a long one, and they still had a lot left to do before they could officially open for business.

"We need a Twitter account and a Facebook group page, and we need to reserve a Doggy Divas website," Roxy said as she typed fast and furiously. Something gooey that dripped on her leg caught her off guard. Kim was trying to squeeze peanut-butter-scented doggy paste into Jazzy's mouth from a tube, but the paste was getting all over Roxy's legs—and her frilly pink-and-white comforter.

"*Eww!* Kim, are you kidding me?" Roxy screeched as she leaped off her bed. The dogs went scurrying, and the tube flew out of Kim's hands. Gobs of brown goo squirted all over Roxy's laptop, copies of the agenda, and the sweater that Georgia was knitting.

"Kim! You ruined this sweater—and I was almost finished!" Georgia started wiping the goop onto Kim's jeans. They were already stained with all sorts of dog fluids. "I wanted to sell it at school tomorrow, but now I'm going to have to stay up all night making a brand-new one."

Kim pulled baby wipes out of her bag and tried to clean the mess on the bed, the sweater, her jeans, and Roxy's legs. But the more she wiped, the more the goo smeared. Roxy tried to stay calm. This was why Roxy and Liz hadn't been friends with Kim—she was just too eccentric and dog crazy!

"Okay, everyone, calm down. Georgia, there's stain remover under the sink in the hallway bathroom. Go see if that will help," Roxy said in an attempt to maintain leadership. "Kim, get off my bed so I can strip it and get the sheets into the laundry. And hand me some baby wipes so I can take care of my computer."

"I'm really sorry, Roxy," Kim said. "I wanted to surprise you guys. It's a new dog treat that I whipped up myself. I thought maybe we could sell it."

"I don't even think that monkeys at the zoo would eat it!" Georgia called from the bathroom. "It smells like baby vomit mixed with my Uncle Milton's room at the nursing home."

Kim coaxed the dogs out from under the bed and started packing up her things.

"Where are you going?" Roxy asked. She knew they couldn't do this without Kim. "We have more work to do!"

"I'm going home," Kim said quietly. "My mom already gives me enough of a hard time about my dogs. I thought you guys wanted my help."

Georgia walked back into Roxy's room with the sweater draped over her shoulder to dry.

"Where are you going?" she asked as she sat back down on Roxy's naked bed.

"Nowhere!" Roxy interjected. "She's going nowhere. Kim wants to go home, but that's just ridiculous. This was just an honest mistake—right, Georgia?"

Roxy shot her a "Please help me" look and hoped that Georgia would show a little sympathy.

"No, don't go home," Georgia said with a touch of sincerity. Not a lot, but it would do. "We don't know anything about dogs. We need you."

"We do!" Roxy promised. "We really, really do."

"Really?" Kim asked. "I mean, I still don't understand why you even want to do this business. Georgia, you don't care about having friends, and Roxy, you're like famous at school…"

"I care…" Georgia trailed off as she started knitting a new sweater. Roxy couldn't believe how quickly she could get a new one started.

"Famous?" Roxy asked. "I don't know about that."

"I guess I'll stay for now, but…" Kim trailed off.

"But what?" Georgia asked. "Do you have a secret dog-society meeting to get to?"

Kim looked like she was going to cry.

"Georgia!" Roxy cried. "Come on!"

"Okay, I'm sorry," Georgia said. "I can't help it. Kim, please stay. We need you."

"We do," Roxy agreed. "We really need you."

"Okay," Kim sighed. "But can we still sell my dog treat if I work on it some more? I can make it less gooey so it won't be as messy."

Roxy shot Georgia a pleading look that basically meant "Shut up and agree with me!"

"Yes! Of course! Let us know when you have the next batch ready," Roxy said in an attempt to get back to business. "How about we move to the next item on the agenda and come up with everyone's titles and responsibilities?"

"Totally, if we really want to look professional, we need titles. And then we can put them on our business cards."

Georgia pulled her hair back into a tight ponytail and continued. "But, we can't put 'dog whisperer' for Kim or 'sweater maker' for me. That just looks amateurish."

"Well, I didn't realize you were related to Donald Trump, Georgia!" Roxy replied sarcastically.

Obviously I need to be president...

"Since you seem to know so much about business, how do you suggest we come up with our titles?" Roxy asked.

Georgia ignored Roxy's tone. "Well, maybe we should make everyone a vice president of her specialty," Georgia explained. "That's how my dad's company works. He's the vice president of creative services. Someone else is the vice president of operations, and someone else is the vice president of human resources..."

"Who's the president?" Kim asked quietly.

This is gonna be interesting, Roxy thought and held her breath.

"Well, that's the thing. We'll all be vice presidents, so we'll all sorta be the president too," Georgia said. "I think that makes things a lot fairer. And we'll all have titles so everyone will know what we do."

Roxy would never admit it out loud, but even if she was *called* vice president, she technically knew that she'd still run the show. Liz or no Liz, Roxy was still the most popular girl of the three of them.

"Okay. I like it," Roxy said. "So, then I want to be the vice president of public relations. All in favor say 'Aye!'"

The girls sang "Aye" together as Izzy and Jazzy jumped up from the tight, little balls they had twisted themselves into on the floor.

"Then let's call me the vice president of fashion, styling, and artistic events. All in favor give me a big ol' 'Aye!'" Georgia giggled.

The girls shrieked "Aye" while laughing hysterically.

"And I want to be vice president of specialized doggie care, nutrition, and customer service," Kim said with a smile. "If you agree, please say 'Aye.'"

"You're so formal, saying 'Please!'" Georgia laughed and playfully threw a dog treat at Kim. Izzy ran over and gobbled it up immediately.

"Well, do you say 'Aye' or not?" Kim was laughing so hard she could barely get the words out.

"Aaaaayyyyeee!" the girls screamed together. They stood up and started hugging and jumping around the room in celebration. Roxy switched on the radio, and they started dancing in a circle. Kim picked up Izzy and spun her around.

"Okay, girls, what are we waiting for?" Roxy sat down breathlessly on her bed. "Let's send an email to announce we're officially open for business. Tomorrow at lunch, we can start taking appointments for our services. Agreed?"

"Agreed!" Georgia and Kim shrieked as they crowded around Roxy's laptop. Izzy and Jazzy kept licking Roxy's face, making it really hard to type. The girls just burst out laughing. Finally, they got the dogs to calm down and put together the perfect email.

THE DOGGY DIVAS: ROXY'S RULES

To: The World

From: Doggydivas@earthworld.com

Re: The Doggy Divas Is Now Open for Business!

Has the dog-walkers' strike landed you in the doghouse? Does your pooch need a crash course in manners? Is your four-legged friend's style so last year?

The Doggy Divas are here to save the day! We can help your favorite friends regain their pre-strike bounce.

Dog walking, dog bathing, dog training, dog fashion, and makeovers—we do it *all!*

Customized and monogrammed sweaters and homemade organic treats are just a few of our specialties.

Roxy Davis, Georgia Sweeney, and Kim Pierce will treat your dog like royalty. No ego too big or small—we're here to pamper your pooch!

Email, call, text, or find us on Facebook to book your appointment now. Or meet us in person during lunch hour at Monroe Middle School.

For the love of dogs,

Roxy, Kim, and Georgia (the Doggy Divas)

The girls huddled nervously around Roxy. She looked at Georgia and Kim before hitting "Send."

"Divas!" Roxy boomed. "Are we ready?"

The girls all grabbed hands and could feel the nervous energy pulsating through each of them. They vigorously nodded their heads, and with a dramatic pause, Roxy hit "Send."

"Guys, I think we're in business!" Roxy squealed, and Izzy and Jazzy barked in delight. "Let's do this!"

Roxy forgot all about Liz, Jessica, the Fashion Bible—and even Matt Billings—for a second. For the first time that week, Roxy was having fun. She had forgotten how good it felt to laugh. She turned the radio back up and grabbed hands with the other girls. They started dancing and singing again at the top of their lungs. It got so loud that they almost didn't hear the phone ring.

Roxy ran to shut the radio off.

"Oh, my God, you guys!" she screeched. "Oh, my God. Oh, my God. That's my bedroom line! I put my phone number in the email. What if it's our first client?"

The girls all sat down and stared at the phone like it was a futuristic gadget they'd never used before.

"Someone needs to answer!" Georgia cried. "We can't just ignore our very first customer! Roxy, you do it!"

"Okay…why am I shaking?" Roxy cried as she placed the ringing phone in her lap.

Kim threw a dog toy at her.

"Come on, this was your idea—just go for it."

Roxy shut her eyes tight and slowly lifted the phone to her ear. "Good afternoon, Doggy Divas. How can I help you?"

Georgia and Kim put their arms around Roxy as she talked. They were gripping her so tightly that Roxy had to pry their hands away so she could breathe—and concentrate on the call!

"Yes, we are open for business." Roxy's eyes were wide

with excitement. "Yes, we can take an order for a sweater. How big is your dog?"

Georgia raised Jazzy high into the air and swung her around in circles. Kim kissed Izzy on the head.

"Okay, Mrs. Cramden. Your little Princess will look adorable—we guarantee it." Roxy was trying to stay calm, but she really wanted to reach through the phone and give Mrs. Cramden a big hug. "We can have it ready by Friday. Can I interest you in any of our homemade dog treats while I have you on the line?"

Roxy hung up the phone, and Georgia and Kim pounced on her.

"Tell us everything!" they squealed.

"That was a nice touch, offering the dog treats!" Georgia said. "I'm impressed!"

"Do they want them?" Kim asked expectantly. "I can try a new recipe tonight!"

But before Roxy could get a word out, the phone rang again.

"I'm so getting it this time!" Georgia declared and grabbed the phone before anyone could argue with her. "Doggy Divas, can I help you?"

Roxy and Kim both strained their ears to see if they could make out what the person on the other end of the phone was saying.

"Oh, so you're not calling on Doggy Diva business?" Georgia asked slyly. "Can I tell her what this is regarding?"

Roxy's eyes were as big and round as vinyl records.

"No worries. I'll absolutely be sure to tell her you called," Georgia said sweetly. "And I'm sure she can tell you more about the Doggy Divas then too!"

Georgia looked absolutely superior as she hung up the phone.

"How much is it worth for me to tell you who was on the phone?" Georgia asked Roxy with a wink. "Because I'm thinking you at least have to give me your iPod or a pair of those fancy designer boots in your closet if you really want to know!"

"Was it Liz?" Roxy asked with a tinge of fear in her voice. "She wasn't on the email, even though I knew she'd find out all about this immediately. Gossip clings to her like to a magnet."

"No, but wow, look how scared you are of her! I knew it!" Georgia pointed out. "Right, Kim?"

Kim was busy giving Izzy and Jazzy tummy rubs and hadn't paid an ounce of attention to the exchange.

"I'm not scared! I just want to know," Roxy said curtly. "It's my phone line—I have rights here."

"Fine! It was Matt," Georgia said smugly. "What's that all about? Isn't he the reason why you and Liz aren't talking? Besides the fact that she's a wretched, tiara-wearing witch…"

"You're lying!" Roxy shrieked. "Tell me who was really on the phone!"

"I'm not lying. I swear on the sweaters I'm going to knit for the Doggy Divas that it was Matt Billings on the phone. He said he wanted to talk about the note he gave you today and congratulate you on Doggy Divas,"

Georgia said. "I guess he *was* on our mass email, huh? And what note?"

Roxy felt like she was going to faint. Matt was calling her to talk? Was he going to turn Liz in for blackmailing him into being her boyfriend? Now all she needed was for Liz to leave school to start competing in pageants in…oh say, Africa, and life would be great. If Liz was gone, maybe Roxy would take her kiss with Matt in the bakery more seriously. Maybe she did have feelings for him after all that could make them more than friends.

"Earth to Roxy," Georgia interrupted. "Are you going to tell us the deal with Matt? I think that as your new business partners, we do have some right to know."

"Nope, there's nothing to tell," Roxy said. "I'll see you guys in the morning so we can start handing out flyers, and then we'll kick things into high gear at lunch!" Roxy stood up and opened her bedroom door. "Just text me tonight if you think of anything else we need to do."

Georgia raised her eyebrows at Roxy but packed up her stuff anyway. Kim put leashes on Izzy and Jazzy, and gave Roxy an awkward hug.

"What was that for?" Roxy asked as she gently hugged her back.

"Just sorry again about making a mess before," Kim said. "Georgia, I hope you can fix that sweater I got dirty."

Roxy couldn't believe it, but Georgia actually hugged Kim too. It was just one arm and a quick pat on the back, but it was something.

"Don't get used to that," Georgia said with a laugh as she walked out of the room with Kim and the dogs behind her. "Good night, Roxy. Don't stay up too late whispering sweet nothings to your boyfriend, Matt Billings!"

"Shut up!" Roxy squealed and slammed her bedroom door shut. She couldn't help but smile as she heard the girls run down the stairs and out the front door.

I think I'll let Matt sweat it out tonight and catch up with him tomorrow at school, Roxy thought to herself as she put new sheets on her bed and sprayed every inch of her room with perfume. The stench from Kim, her dogs, and the treats were going to be hard to get used to—and to get rid of!

DOGGY CONFESSIONAL
JAZZY

Kim's treats are gross. I don't want to be mean, but they taste like dirt. So, I did what any dog looking to score good treats would do. I stole some from Matt's backpack after school.

He didn't notice. He was arguing with Liz. She wanted Matt to defriend Roxy on Facebook. When Matt said he wouldn't do it, Liz went wild. I guess no one ever taught her "no" in obedience school.

I just wanted treats—not drama!

Chapter Eight

THE NEXT MORNING, ROXY woke up feeling like she had forgotten to do something. She'd finished all her homework, so she needed a minute to figure out what was nagging her.

Oh, right. I didn't call Matt back, she realized as she peeled her sleeping mask off her eyes and plucked the earplugs from her ears. The mask was labeled "Beauty Queen" and was a hand-me-down from Liz. She had gotten it in a gift bag at a pageant, but she applied special moisturizer every night to keep her skin smooth and thought the mask would irritate her complexion.

Roxy had taken the mask happily because rays of sun poked through her shades and woke her up every morning. The earplugs were a new part of her sleep regimen. Those annoying dog walkers had the nerve to start protesting and marching through the neighborhood at 5 a.m. The previous night, Roxy's dad had brought home a pair of earplugs for everyone in the family.

Should I call Matt back now? Roxy wondered as she sneaked into her parents' room to see if her mom had anything her daughter could borrow. *This is where I need Liz. She always knows the right thing to do when it comes to boys.*

Roxy found a cute, navy-blue tank dress in her mom's closet that looked nothing like anything in the Fashion Bible. What she wore didn't matter, now that the dogs had destroyed the notebook, but Roxy didn't want to take any chances. She went back to her room, put on a thin, black belt, and dressed up the look with a pair of ankle boots.

Turning her bedroom into an imaginary runway, Roxy sashayed across the floor a few times. She couldn't have a repeat of the other day and end up in her gym shoes again. When Roxy was confident she could spend the day in the boots comfortably, she tied her hair up in a high ponytail and met her dad in the car.

Roxy gulped as her dad dropped her off in the front of the school. Dogs were still running all over the lawn. Principal West was handing out detentions left and right to anyone who had a dog with them. She didn't see Liz or Matt anywhere, but Kim and Georgia anxiously greeted Roxy as she stepped out of the car.

Georgia had a stack of bright flyers printed with all of the Doggy Divas' information that she had made using her dad's copy machine the night before. Kim hugged a box to her chest, while Dixie, Izzy, and Jazzy, who was still owner-less, sat by her feet.

"'Morning, divas!" Roxy laughed as she exited the car and blew her dad a kiss. "What's in the box?"

"I have tons of treats lying around, so I thought it would be a nice touch to give a baggie full of them to anyone that makes an appointment today," Kim said hesitantly. "I forgot to text you. Is that okay?"

"Okay? It's *great!* I love that idea," Roxy exclaimed. "Let's start handing out these flyers. Just, uh, try to stay away from Liz and those girls if you can…"

Georgia scoffed as she dropped a stack of flyers in the middle of a group of seventh graders sitting on the ground.

"You look pretty today…" Georgia said. "Trying to impress anyone? Maybe his name rhymes with 'cat'?"

"There's a cat?" Kim asked fearfully as she stapled a few flyers onto a tree. "Izzy hates cats, and I'm more of a dog person, as you know…"

Roxy and Georgia burst out laughing. The bell rang just as they handed out their last flyer.

"Okay, girls—I'll see you at lunch," Roxy said as she ran off to homeroom. "Text me if anyone asks about the Doggy Divas before then!"

The rest of the morning was a blur. Roxy felt like a celebrity in every class because everyone was bombarding her with questions about the Doggy Divas. It was like she was at a press conference. So many kids were desperate to pass their responsibility on to a new dog walker.

Plus, their usual dog walkers didn't knit sweaters nor bake homemade treats nor give their pups spa treatments, so the Doggy Divas was an instant hit. Even teachers stopped Roxy in the hall to ask for a flyer or more information. Roxy had only printed up a few business cards on her computer, and they were gone by the time she got to lunch.

More dogs than students were roaming the school grounds, and the dog walkers were still striking outside the school yard. Roxy didn't see an end in sight for this battle.

Maybe the Doggy Divas will make us lots of money! Roxy smiled to herself as she scanned the crowd for Kim and Georgia. *I can buy a whole new wardrobe.*

Roxy plopped down on the grassy lawn by the fence that was now the Doggy Divas' designated lunch spot. She hugged her knees to her chest, put on her sunglasses, and tried to soak up some sun before the other girls arrived. Roxy was trying to think of tactful ways to propose giving Kim a makeover when she was startled by the commotion going on around her.

"Me first! My mom is going to kill me if the dog poops in the house one more time!"

"Hey—quit elbowing me. I was ahead of you!"

"Get out of my way. If you take my appointment, I'll never talk to you again!"

"M-o-v-e it!"

A mob of classmates had surrounded Roxy and were fighting for her attention. Roxy had only seen this sort of commotion on *Entertainment Tonight* when crazy fans and paparazzi tried to get a celebrity to notice them at the Academy Awards.

What in the world is going on here? Roxy stood up and looked around for Kim and Georgia.

"Excuse me. I need an appointment with the Doggy Divas more than you do!"

"Uh, no. I think I need one a little bit more than you."

Roxy couldn't believe it. Everyone was crowding her because of the Doggy Divas? She was pulling out her appointment book when help arrived in the nick of time.

"Everyone get out of the way! Make three straight lines, or you won't get an appointment!" Georgia commanded as she pushed to the front of the crowd. She was dragging Kim by the hand through the sea of kids and dogs to get to Roxy. "Either you wait in line, or we don't help you. It's as easy as that, people!"

Georgia and Kim dragged over an old picnic table from a few feet away so the girls could sit side by side on the bench and each have her own potential clients line up in front of her.

"How did this happen?" Roxy asked as she sat down next to Georgia. "I don't know if we're prepared for this kind of demand!"

Georgia flashed a big smile as she removed Dixie from her carrier and sat the dog on her lap. "We hit on a million-dollar idea here! Everyone wants the best for their dogs," she explained. "It'll be fine. I promise."

Kim got up and placed Jazzy on Roxy's lap. "I think it'll be a nice touch if we each hold a dog," Kim said as she gave each dog a treat and sat back down with Izzy. "People won't trust us unless they see how much we love dogs."

The line wrapped all the way around to the front of the lunch area by where Liz and her crew sat. A knot formed in Roxy's stomach because she knew there was no way Liz would ignore a crowd around Roxy's table—especially since she wasn't invited. But Roxy just kept scheduling dog-walking appointments while Georgia took orders for sweaters. Kim answered questions about care and training while using Izzy as a model. Roxy had absolutely no idea how they were going to manage walking all these dogs, but there was no turning back now.

"Um, excuse me. I'd like to buy two sweaters, please," a deep voice whispered in Roxy's ear.

"Oh, you need to talk to Georgia…" Roxy choked on her words as she turned to see Matt standing over her. Roxy gulped. She hoped he wasn't mad that she hadn't called him back the night before. She noticed her hands were so sweaty that she could barely hold her pen and wondered why she was so nervous.

"Hey," she said shyly. "I'm sorta busy—can you believe this line? And you shouldn't be here. What if Liz sees and gets you kicked off the team?"

Matt sat on the bench next to her. Georgia shot her a "What's going on here?" look while an oblivious Kim happily taught a group of girls the proper way to bathe a dog. She had Izzy flat on her back and was poking and prodding the poor dog's most sensitive areas.

"I'll handle Liz. I'm really proud of you. This is amazing," he said. "But I really do want to buy two sweaters—one for my aunt's dog and one for Banjo. That one will have to be macho, of course!"

Roxy was too distracted to hear what he was saying. Their appointment calendar was almost filled for the entire month! She couldn't believe it.

"What? Your aunt is a dog?" Roxy said absentmindedly.

Matt laughed. "No, my aunt *has* a dog," he said. "A cute little terrier! She gets cold in the winter."

"You need to talk to Georgia, but I'll make sure that she gives you VIP treatment," Roxy said. "I, um…I'm sorry I didn't get to call you last night. Things were busy. You should go now. Liz *will* ruin your athletic future. She doesn't joke about her threats."

Roxy's heart was doing flip-flops. She was about to flash him a sincere smile when Liz sneaked up behind them and linked her arm through Matt's. Little Roxie's head popped out of the sparkly pink carrier that was slung over Liz's shoulder. Matt looked helpless and confused. Roxy wanted to wipe that smug smile right off Liz's face.

"I'm sorry, Matt, but did you mistake this Roxy for my dog?" Liz asked slyly as she gripped Matt's arm tighter. "Weren't you just telling me how much cuter my little Roxie was than any other Roxy we know?"

Roxy actually felt bad for Matt. He looked defeated. She knew how hard it was to stand up to Liz, so she didn't expect him to defend her until he was really sure Liz wasn't going to do something bad—like tell his coach lies about how he'd cheated on last year's math placement exam.

"Um, I need a sweater," Matt said sheepishly. "That's why I'm here."

"You need a sweater from these losers?" Liz said loudly. The crowd went silent. Georgia and Kim looked up at Roxy, their eyes wide with fear. "It's the Three Musketeers—Miss Boyfriend Stealer, Miss Loud Mouth, and my favorite, Miss Doggie Doo. Great team. Especially since Roxy didn't even know their names until she became desperado for new friends!"

"Look, Liz—you're not welcome on this side of the lunch tables." Georgia stood up on her chair. "Just go back to taping your Fashion Bible back together and leave us alone."

"Nobody tells me where I am and am not welcome at this school," Liz responded furiously.

She turned her attention back to Roxy. "How do you like sitting here? Was it worth double-crossing me?"

Matt let go of Liz's grip and took a step back. In a blink, he somehow managed to disappear into the crowd.

"Well, you know what?" Liz asked sweetly. "I think little Roxie could use a new dog walker. And a sweater. Maybe even some dog treats. Sign me up!"

Roxy looked over at Kim and Georgia in a panic. There was no way they could accept business from Liz. She would make their lives even more unbearable—if that was possible. The second Liz handed them money, she became a Doggy Divas client, and they would have to obey every single one of her awful demands. That would be Liz's sneaky way of blackmailing them—just like she was blackmailing Matt.

"Sorry," Georgia interjected. "We're booked solid."

Liz looked over her shoulder at the long line of desperate students and their dogs waiting to make an appointment.

"Oh, really?" she sneered. "You're going to tell everyone else who's waiting the same thing? That doesn't seem very business savvy to me."

"We have the right to refuse service to anyone we want. It's in the local business guidelines," Roxy said officially. She didn't even know if "local business guidelines" existed, but it sounded like something she heard her dad say on the phone to his clients. "We're very sorry about that."

Roxy realized that everyone—including Kim and Georgia—was staring at her and Liz. She and Liz were practically Monroe Middle School's own reality show. *How many more days in a row can I star in the Roxy and Liz Showdown?* she wondered. Little Roxie started whimpering from her carrier, desperate for Roxy to give her some affection. *Poor little Roxie—I wonder if she understands how mean her mom is.*

"I'd like to see you try to explain those guidelines to Principal West," Liz said arrogantly. "I don't think those rules apply at school. You are an officially sanctioned school club, right? I mean, you wouldn't be able to conduct business on school grounds otherwise, as I'm sure you know."

"Of course we know," Georgia interrupted. "We followed all the rules. If you want to wait in line for an appointment, fine, but we're pretty booked."

Roxy watched Liz's face carefully. Roxy knew there was no way Liz actually believed them. Of course they weren't an official school club. But, if taking care of little Roxie would shut Liz up for now, they really had no choice. It was going to be awful, because Roxy knew without a doubt that Liz would treat the Doggy Divas like they were her own personal servants.

"What types of services do you want?" Roxy asked in her most professional-sounding voice. She opened the pink notebook she was using to keep track of appointments and looked at Liz expectantly. "There's a long line behind you, so what will it be? Walking? Grooming? A training session? Do you want to place a sweater order?"

"Everything. I want my Roxie walked, groomed, and trained, and I'll take three sweaters—a rush job on those," Liz chirped. "I assume you take credit cards?"

"Um, no. If that's a problem, you can take your business elsewhere," Georgia chimed in.

Liz gave her a nasty look and finished making her appointment. "I'll just have my mom write you a check," she quipped. "I'll see you Doggy DoDos at my house tomorrow."

Liz spun on her sparkly kitten heels, flipped her blond hair over her shoulder, and waltzed away like she was leaving the stage at a pageant. A few students were still waiting around to make an appointment, but lunch time was almost over and everyone was heading back into the main building. Georgia and Kim stared at Roxy, waiting for her to say something about what had just happened.

"She thinks she's queen of this school," Georgia said

with a huff. "But, we're not going to let her walk all over us! She's just jealous she didn't think of the Doggy Divas first."

Roxy just sat there silently. This was a nightmare.

"Yeah, Roxy, so what if Liz Craft is our new client? She's giving us money," Kim said meekly. "We have a whole calendar filled with appointments. Do we really care that she's one of them? There's nothing that she can do to hurt us as long as we do a good job."

Roxy slumped down and put her chin on the picnic table. The girls kept going on about how Liz couldn't keep them down.

"Can you two just shut up for one second?" Roxy barked. Even she was surprised by how angry she sounded. "This *is* bad. This *is* a problem, and it *does* matter that Liz just hired us."

Kim and Georgia started to gather their things. They didn't say a word, but Roxy knew by the looks on their faces that she had hurt their feelings.

"Look, guys, I'm sorry," Roxy said. "Liz used to be my best friend, and now she's my client. I'm still trying to get used to the idea."

"Don't worry. We're in this together," Georgia said. "But maybe we should make sure we have all the right permission from Principal West to do this."

Kim nodded in agreement while feeding all the leftover treats to a pack of strays that had found their way over to her. The girls finished packing up their supplies and were about to head back to the building when they realized that Principal West was on his way over to them.

"Uh-oh," Kim whispered. "Maybe we *are* in trouble!"

The girls sat up straight. Kim grabbed Izzy and tried to stuff the little dog into her tote bag. Izzy, of course, was having none of it. She kept popping her head up and sticking her tongue out so far that she looked like she was smiling.

"Hello, girls!" Principal West said hurriedly. It was hot and he was dressed in a three-piece suit, so he kept mopping his shiny forehead with a handkerchief as sweat slid down his face. Roxy noticed that Liz was watching them from a distance. Jessica was with her too.

"Don't worry. I already told your teachers you might be late. I need to talk to you." He sat down and started petting Izzy behind the ears.

Roxy, Georgia, and Kim grabbed each other's hands under the table.

"As you girls know, the school is quite a mess because of the dog walkers' strike. We have dogs on campus, in classrooms…and 'Bring Your Dog to School Day' was somewhat of a disaster," Principal West explained. "It's been brought to my attention that you gals have started a dog-walking business. Now while I applaud your initiative, student businesses of any kind are strictly forbidden."

Roxy, Georgia, and Kim all looked at each other with their eyes wide.

"But I'm willing to turn a blind eye because we just

can't have this many dogs roaming around school. The board of health commissioners will close down this school if they find out," Principal West continued. "So when Liz Craft informed me that you girls had started this business, I was a bit surprised.

"Under normal circumstances, I would have had to stop it immediately. But if you girls can promise me that it won't interfere with your studies, I'll even allow you to arrive at school a few minutes late and leave a few minutes early to tend to your dog walking. Does that sound good?"

Izzy was playing tug-of-war with Principal West and his handkerchief. He nervously tried to pull it back as she held on tighter and let out a tiny growl.

The girls nodded their heads in unison. Principal West finally relented and let Izzy keep his handkerchief.

"Okay, now get to class!"

The girls stayed back as Principal West walked back into the building, mopping up his sweaty head with the sleeve of his jacket.

"Oh, my God!" Georgia laughed. "I think he's wearing a toupee!" His hair appeared to be on more of a right angle than when he'd left the building. "I'm dying for Izzy to just yank it off one day!"

They were laughing so hard that Roxy thought she was going to pee in her pants.

"So, wait…I don't get it," Kim said, getting back to business. "Liz told on us, but Principal West didn't care?"

"I guess so," Georgia said. "Let's just look at this as a

point for the Doggy Divas! Maybe Liz isn't as mighty as she thinks.

"You know what? I'm not so sure about that," Roxy said with authority creeping back into her voice. "We have to be careful and plan ahead. Kim, can we meet at your house a little earlier today to get all the business in?"

Both girls nodded.

"We need to discuss our plans for when we start walking dogs tomorrow anyway," Roxy said. "I'll see you all later. Consider it our first mandatory, emergency Doggy Diva meeting!"

DOGGY CONFESSIONAL
LITTLE ROXIE

I think it's so cute the way Matt and Roxy look at each other. I can tell there is something between them—I can actually smell it!

Poor Liz just wants everyone to like her, even if she doesn't deserve it. I know she learns how to make people like her at pageant camp. I watch her practice in the mirror all the time. She says things like "You're such a peach!" or "Why, aren't you just a living doll!" It's embarrassing to watch!

Chapter Nine

THAT AFTERNOON, ROXY WAS still taking dog-walking orders from students—and teachers. Word about the Doggy Divas had spread faster than the rumor Roxy and Liz had started a year earlier that they were going on a double date with royal princes visiting from a foreign country.

Everyone thought Roxy was a dog expert when she didn't really know a thing about dogs. That was Kim's department. Roxy actually panicked when she realized that tomorrow morning she would have to put dogs on their leashes and pick up their poop. She'd learned from Liz to always "smile and fake it." That was Liz's motto when it came to pageants—and everything else in life.

I'm sure gonna have to fake it when I show up on Liz's doorstep tomorrow morning, Roxy realized as she walked up the pebbled driveway that led to Kim's house.

She looked down at her BlackBerry to confirm that she was at the right place. She hated to admit it, but she'd never really thought about where Kim lived. And she'd never expected her to live in a mansion! It was even nicer than Liz's place.

Roxy softly tapped the gold knocker. It was so

heavy and sparkly that she was fairly sure it had to be solid gold.

Or maybe it's filled with chocolate! Roxy laughed to herself.

"Hello!" A woman in a bright-pink bathrobe answered the door with a big smile on her face. "I'm so sorry to meet you like this. Mr. Pierce and I have a benefit to attend tonight, and I'm starting to get dressed early. Are you Georgia? Or Roxy? I'm Kim's mom."

"Hi, I'm Roxy..." Roxy was stunned. Kim's gorgeous mom was going to a benefit? Then why did Kim dress in ratty clothes every day and never brush her hair and smell like garbage? "It's really nice to meet you. Is Kim home?"

"Izzy—nooooooooo!" Kim yelled at the top of her lungs. Roxy and Mrs. Pierce ran to the stairs just in time for a soaking-wet Izzy to splash them with a soapy mess of water and bubbles.

"Um, I guess she's home," Roxy said with a small smile. For a split second, she forgot that Liz was her enemy and almost pulled out her phone to text Liz about this scene. Roxy felt a pang of loneliness for Liz. She would never believe that Kim was rich—and that she let dogs destroy her beautiful home.

"I'm sorry! I forgot to close the bathroom door during her bath..." Kim raced down the stairs. Roxy followed her while Mrs. Pierce went to grab some paper towels from the kitchen. Roxy and Kim found Izzy rolling around on the living-room couch, desperately trying to dry off. The little dog was covered in soap at least an inch thick, and her usually black hair was sticky, matted, and white as snow. Kim lunged for Izzy, but the dog leaped off the couch and ran between Kim's legs. Soapy water drenched the carpet, the stairs, and everything in Izzy's path.

"Kimberly Naomi Pierce! Get your butt in the dining room immediately!"

"Uh-oh," Kim said with fear clouding over face. "Whenever my mom uses my middle name, I'm dead meat."

The girls ran back into the dining room to find Mrs. Pierce lying flat on her back in a puddle, having slipped on the dog's soapy trail of water. Her bathrobe was soaking wet, and the newspapers that had been in recycling bins in the kitchen were now strewn in a million pieces all over the dining room. Izzy sat at the top of the stairs barking her head off. The two teacup-sized stray Chihuahuas bounced around behind her.

Georgia showed up just in time for the show. She stood in the doorway taking in the scene, her eyes wide with confusion. For the first time in her entire life, she was speechless—but only for a fleeting moment.

"Are there hidden cameras here?" Georgia asked in shock. "Is this a practical joke? Are we going to be on TV?"

Roxy ran over to stand by Georgia. She couldn't decide if she was more alarmed that Mrs. Pierce was about to lose her robe in front of everyone or that no one else in the Pierce family shared Kim's love of dogs. Roxy had just assumed it was a genetic thing. And then she realized that Kim was probably an outcast at home too.

The Chihuahuas were jumping on Izzy's back and trying to eat bubbles off her fur. Still soaking wet, Izzy kept attempting to shake herself dry. This, of course, splashed the Chihuahuas. They ran down the stairs to get away from Izzy—and to take refuge under Mrs. Pierce's robe.

"Kim," her mom said calmly. "Where did these Chihuahuas come from?"

"I'm sorry, Mom, but Izzy got into the garbage on our walk home from school, and that's where these Chihuahuas were hiding and, well, they recognized me from school. Izzy smelled like spaghetti so I decided to give her a bath, and the Chihuahuas just aren't used to the house yet..."

"Kim, these dogs will not have the opportunity to get used to our house. No more dogs!" her mom said while squeezing water out of her robe like a mop. "We'll talk more about this later."

The Chihuahuas nipped at the bottom of Mrs. Pierce's bathrobe—making it rather difficult and potentially embarrassing for her to stand up straight.

"Come on, guys," Kim said quietly. She snapped her fingers, and the dogs followed her up the stairs. Roxy and Georgia went right behind them.

"I can't believe this place!" Georgia mouthed to Roxy as they walked up the marble stairs and down a long, picturesque hallway filled with artwork to Kim's room. The bathroom—which was strewn with towels and wet doggy footprints—actually had a loveseat. And Kim's room was double the size of Roxy's *parents'* room.

Don't they have a maid? Roxy wondered as they sat down. She wrinkled her nose in disgust and noticed that Georgia did the same.

Kim's room reeked of dog treats, and every inch of the black, shaggy carpet was covered in dog hair. Kim's walls were a collage of posters, charts, news clippings, and photographs about anything and everything to do with canines. She had more dog toys, dog beds, and dog food displayed than most pet stores had in stock. Roxy sat on a dog pillow shaped like a bone, while Georgia grabbed one that was shaped like a candy bar. Kim snuggled up with the dogs in her bed. Izzy was already curled up in a tight little ball.

"Kim, you have not one, not two, not three, but *four* showerheads in that swanky bathroom of yours, and you can't take a shower every morning?" Georgia asked. "I mean…"

"Georgia!" Roxy shot her a look. "You don't have to say everything that instantly pops into your brain."

"I'm sorry. I just…well, I just really thought that everyone in Kim's house was a dog freak too," Georgia said quietly. "I was half expecting Lassie or Snoopy to answer the door."

Even Kim couldn't help but laugh.

"Yeah, well, my mom doesn't think that dogs are a very ladylike hobby," Kim said while giving the Chihuahuas a cue to jump through her belt like a hoop. "But dogs have always understood me and accepted me. Most people don't."

As soon as Kim said that, Roxy felt really bad about

all the times during the previous year when she and Liz had tortured Kim because she smelled like kibble or spent lunchtime rescuing strays.

"Well, then, that's why you're the perfect vice president of specialized doggie care, nutrition, and customer service," Georgia said sincerely. "I have a dog and don't know a thing compared to you!"

Kim blushed so deeply that her face, neck, and arms turned crimson.

"Okay, let's get down to business then," Roxy said. "Item Number One—Liz Craft."

"Where are our agendas?" Georgia asked as she took out her knitting bag and started working on a sweater. The Chihuahuas immediately started trying to grab the needles from her hands. "I thought they were a nice touch."

Kim got up and placed all the dogs in a playpen filled with even more toys.

"Well, with just two items—Liz and our dog-walking schedule—I was trying to be eco-friendly!" Roxy said in an annoyed voice. She didn't like it when Georgia made her feel like she'd done something wrong.

"What are we going to do about Liz?" Kim asked. "I mean, do we really have to take her on as a client?"

"Yes," Roxy said confidently. "We shouldn't really turn anyone away. It's not fair. But we can't let her think we're worried. If we drop her as a client, we'll look like she got to us and we care what she thinks."

Georgia let out a snort as she clacked away on her latest

doggie sweater. She had ten to finish by the end of the week. So far, her sweaters were the most requested service from the Doggy Divas besides, of course, dog walking.

"So what do we do?" Georgia asked. "Liz Craft will do anything to get her way."

"We'll have to train her—like a dog," Kim piped in. "Dogs are very responsive to repetition. They learn by hearing the same command or doing the same trick over and over. We'll just have to be nice and emotionless every day, the exact same way, when she's around. As mean as it sounds, we have to treat her like a dog."

Okay, one of these days, we're going to have to get Kim to a mall and introduce her to the two-legged species, but for now, she's got a point...

Roxy was shocked at the endless knowledge Kim had about dogs. She herself loved clothes, but she barely knew a thing about the fashion industry. Listening to Kim was impressive—and overwhelming sometimes!

"If we're training her, then let's get a muzzle to put over her yappy mouth," Georgia suggested.

The girls burst out laughing.

"Okay...let's move to our final order of business. Dog-walking duties begin tomorrow morning, bright and early!" Roxy exclaimed.

Kim and Georgia groaned, but Roxy ignored them.

"Girls, we have to start our day at 6 a.m. We have fifteen dogs to walk before school and fifteen to walk after school," Roxy dictated. "I think five dogs each should be fine, but we need to split it up based on the dogs that are closest to our houses."

They each picked their five dogs, and Roxy had no choice but to take little Roxie. The Crafts lived closest to her, and one of Liz's "special" requests was for Roxy to be her walker. For now, at least, Roxy was willing to go along with whatever Liz wanted so they could get this business off the ground without Liz ruining it more than she'd already tried.

"You guys, please be easy to reach after I pick up little Roxie!" Roxy begged. "What if Liz puts a video camera in her—like one of those nanny cams or something? I may need you guys to inspect her!"

"Don't worry. There's nowhere inside a dog that she could fit such a thing…" Kim started to explain. Roxy and Georgia rolled their eyes, and Kim trailed off.

"Oh, wait! I almost forgot!" Kim jumped up and ran over to her closet. She pulled out a box and handed Roxy and Georgia each a sack with plastic bags to scoop up dog poop, hand sanitizer, and dog treats.

"Think of these three things as your 'canine kit.' Use them for every walk," Kim said. "Leaving poop on the street is against the law, and you want to make sure your hands are clean at all times. Treats are a way of earning a dog's trust and rewarding him for good behavior, but don't use them as bribes. Dogs are very smart creatures."

Georgia sniffed one of the treats and made a face. "Are we going to get a lecture from you about the proper care of dogs every time we meet?" she asked.

"Yes, we are," Roxy jumped in. "I think we need Kim to teach us because I really don't know all that much about dogs—at least you guys each have one—so yes, Kim will be teaching us."

Kim beamed with pride. Roxy realized that Kim must not get many compliments on her dog knowledge—especially from her mom.

"Okay, girls, we have a big day of dog walking ahead of us. I say this meeting is adjourned so we can go home and get some much-needed beauty rest!"

DOGGY CONFESSIONAL
IZZY

Was Kim adopted at the local shelter like I was? She sure is a different breed from her parents. Kim is sort of...well, like a mutt. And her mother is a regal top breed!

So what if Kim isn't perfect. Like all mutts, Kim has a heart of gold. She takes exceptional care of us and never gets mad when we do things like poop on the couch. We don't mean to—sometimes we can't help ourselves!

Kim has to put up with so much from the bullies at school that we don't want anyone else making her feel worse—like her parents. We like to protect her whenever we can, just like she protects us.

Chapter Ten

THE NEXT MORNING, ROXY popped up out of bed almost a full hour before her alarm clock rang. She was so anxious about managing five dogs—including little Roxie—that her dreams during the night had been filled with images of ten-foot-tall Yorkie-Poos that all looked like little Roxie.

She stretched her arms over her head and tried to decide on the perfect dog-walking outfit. At least she didn't have to worry about running into Jessica dressed in anything similar. And there was no way that Jessica would be out and about before the sun was up.

Roxy was trying hard not to think about showing up at Liz's house in about an hour. She could picture the smug and satisfied look on Liz's face when she opened the door and saw Roxy, the "hired help," standing there. Liz had the same superior look plastered across her face whenever she tormented her housekeeper by forcing the poor woman to make Liz's grilled-cheese sandwich over and over until she got the crust just crispy enough. Roxy was nervous enough about walking five dogs; it would be a lot easier if little Roxie wasn't one of them.

She glanced at the clock. It was now 5:30 a.m., and

she was expected at the Goldman household by 6 a.m. to pick up Tyler, a St. Bernard. Roxy looked at the rest of the carefully organized and printed-out schedule she had made for herself and the rest of the girls. After picking up Tyler, Roxy had to retrieve Chloe the Pomeranian, Precious the cocker spaniel, Horton the corgi, and finally little Roxie.

Guess I'm saving the best for last today, Roxy sighed as she pulled on a pair of cropped, hot-pink yoga pants, a gray hoodie, and sneakers. She didn't have any experience in dressing for dog walking—even with all the time that she had spent with little Roxie. Liz did very little to take care of little Roxie, other than dressing her in ridiculous outfits, toting her around, and loving all the attention the tiny dog attracted.

Roxy grabbed Kim's canine kit and was about to head out the door when she decided that, as vice president of public relations, it was her duty to update the Doggy Divas Twitter feed first thing every morning.

@MissDoggyDiva: Just out for our morning walk! What R U waiting for? Call us! Ur dog will thank u!

Then Roxy flipped open her cell phone to text her business partners and pump them up in honor of their first official morning of dog walking.

To: Georgia cell, Kim cell
From: Roxy cell

"Good morning, divas! I can feel it—this morning will put the Doggy Divas on the map! But, if U want to walk little Roxie for me, I'll pay you $1,000. XO, R"

Roxy quietly shut the front door behind her so she wouldn't wake anyone. She had casually mentioned to her mom that she was helping out the neighborhood by walking dogs during the strike. Eventually her mom would realize that her daughter was a full-fledged business owner, but for now Roxy didn't want to have to explain her new friends and the lack of her old ones.

Maybe I'll wait to tell her when we make the cover of Entrepreneur *magazine or Warren Buffett buys a stake in the Doggy Divas!* Roxy laughed to herself as she ran up the walkway of the Goldman house and tried to stop from shaking with nerves. Tyler started barking before she even rang the doorbell.

"Tyler, quiet!" Mrs. Goldman commanded. She was wearing a yellow-and-blue kimono that was too short. Roxy tried to keep her focus on Mrs. Goldman's face. "Roxy, you're a lifesaver. He's been going nuts ever since Carla decided to strike. The whole thing is just a mess!"

Roxy stood there paralyzed with fear. Standing on all fours, Tyler was almost as tall as she was and probably weighed twice as much. Her dream seemed to be coming true as a real-life nightmare. This dog was going to drag her all over the neighborhood!

"Um, no problem, Mrs. Goldman," Roxy said brightly and hoped Mrs. Goldman couldn't hear her heart pounding through her chest. "I'm going to pick up the other dogs for a nice little walk, and I'll bring him back as soon as possible."

"Roxy, dear, is Chloe one of the dogs you'll be walking this morning?"

Roxy nodded but couldn't understand why in the world Mrs. Goldman would care.

"Okay, well, no problem, but just make sure that they're separated. Don't let them walk side by side, and you'll be fine."

Roxy's eyes widened as she grabbed Tyler's leash. He was sweet at first and actually let Roxy take the lead. But when they approached Chloe's house, Tyler began whimpering in fear and refused to budge. Finally Roxy managed to drag him up to the door, where she knocked lightly.

"Who is it?" asked a high-pitched voice.

"It's Roxy Davis with the Doggy Divas!" Roxy sang. "Is Chloe ready for her walk?"

The door swung open, and a tiny Pomeranian bounced outside. Her owner, Mrs. Rogers, scooped her up before she got too far.

"Oh, look, Chloe! Tyler is here—you have a friend for your walk!" Mrs. Rogers cooed.

Tyler whimpered, and Roxy started to panic. Tyler was a giant in comparison to little Chloe, so why was he so scared of this little puff of white fluff?

"Roxy, you take good care of my sweet little princess!" Mrs. Rogers begged. "Chloe, you be a good girl for Roxy, and Mommy will have a treatie-weatie waiting for you when you get back!"

The minute Mrs. Rogers closed the door, angelic little Chloe turned into an evil little devil—with her sights set on tormenting poor Tyler. Chloe growled and nipped at Tyler's feet. At first, Roxy thought it was funny to watch such a little dog intimidate a giant one. But when she broke a nail trying to keep them apart, she stopped laughing.

Roxy barely managed to drag them along to pick up Precious and Horton. After that, it was better having two dogs between to keep Tyler and Chloe separated. But the next stop was Liz's house, and Roxy couldn't let Liz see that she was having any problem controlling the dogs. Roxy needed Kim's expertise and texted her in a panic. How was she going to get Tyler and Chloe to follow her commands *before* arriving at Liz's house?

To: Kim
From: Roxy

"SOS! Dogs won't behave!. Can't let Liz see! Help!"

Roxy waited a few minutes, but there was no response from Kim. Closing her eyes, Roxy let her mind go blank. Then she inhaled deeply from her belly—just like she had watched her mom do when she practiced yoga in the living room.

I need to get zen—stat!

Roxy opened her eyes and pretended that a pair of invisible hands were pushing her up the front walk to the Crafts' mansion. Roxy was overwhelmed with pangs of nostalgia. She had spent so much time there over the years that the house had practically become her second home.

And now, she and Liz were like strangers, Roxy thought sadly as she rang the doorbell and prayed Mrs. Craft would come to the door instead of Liz.

The Crafts' doorbell played a high-pitched melody that lasted until the front door swung open. The noise was too much for Chloe, Tyler, Precious, and Horton to bear, and they all started howling and crying while trying desperately to run away. Roxy had officially lost control.

"Stop it, now!" Roxy begged.

Without missing a beat, Tyler lifted his leg and peed all over the Crafts' front mat.

"*Tyler!*" Roxy screamed. "*Bad dog!*"

As if on cue, Liz flung open the front door with little Roxie nestled in her arms. Liz looked Roxy up and down, but her eyes went wide with shock when she noticed the growing puddle under Roxy's feet.

"Um, wow. Isn't it your job as a dog walker to make sure the dogs *don't* pee on the house?" Liz scoffed without even saying hello. "There are paper towels in the kitchen."

Roxy stared at Liz as if Liz had just told her that little green men were cooking breakfast in there. "I can't leave all these dogs here to go get towels—unless you want to watch the dogs?"

Liz stomped off to get the paper towels and threw them at Roxy when she returned. "I'm already docking $5 off your pay. You just destroyed my personal property."

Roxy wanted to slam the door shut and tell Liz she could just shove it. Wasn't the mat her parents' personal property? Roxy managed to clean the pee up with no stain left behind and remembered what Kim said yesterday about "training" Liz.

"Well, if that's what it'll take to give you a satisfactory experience with the Doggy Divas, then okay," Roxy said as she took little Roxie from Liz's arms. "Is there anything special I need to know about little Roxie before we get going on her walk?"

"Just know that I have spies, and I know everything," Liz raged with her blue eyes lit up in anger. "Every mistake you make—everyone at school will know all about it. And don't think I won't dock another dollar for every minute you're late to bring her back. You have fifteen minutes."

Liz slammed the door in her face, and Roxy stuck her tongue out in a fit of rage. She walked so angrily that she wasn't paying attention to the dogs when Tyler stuck his big nose in her pocket and pulled out all of the dog treats. Immediately, the dogs tackled them—and pulled Roxy down in the chaos.

To make it even worse, the bag of poop she had been collecting throughout the walk went flying. The smell of doggy doo wafted toward her, and she started to gag. Roxy willed herself not to throw up.

"Uh, missing something?" a deep voice asked from above.

Roxy opened one eye. A hand was stretched out in front of her.

"Roxy? Are you okay?" The voice was a lot more urgent and worried now. "Let me help you up."

Roxy slowly opened both eyes—it was Matt Billings!

"Matt, what are you doing here?" Roxy rubbed her eyes and looked around. She was so confused. "Where are the dogs?"

"Don't worry, Roxy," Matt laughed. "The dogs are fine. This troublemaker Chloe is torturing Tyler while everyone else is enjoying their treats. I see Chloe and Tyler get into it at the dog park all the time."

"Where did you come from?" Roxy asked.

"I'd just started my morning run when I noticed a doggie pileup over here. I thought that was you underneath them all, but I wasn't sure," Matt said while helping Roxy get untangled. "Did you kidnap all these puppies?"

"Matt! I didn't steal these dogs. Don't you remember that I have a dog-walking business?" Roxy blushed.

"I'm kidding. Remember when we used to be able to joke?" he asked softly, and his eyes clouded over for a second. "I still have to hire you to walk Banjo."

"I don't know…you may want Kim to take care of him instead of me," Roxy said while quickly taking a head count to make sure none of the dogs had escaped. "She's much better at handling these guys."

"I don't know about that," Matt said. "I want you."

Roxy smiled and didn't say anything in return. She felt lighter than air.

"Well, well, well! What do we have going on here, Roxy?" Liz's voice boomed out of nowhere. "Flirting and socializing is *not* what I pay you to do. I think that's at least another five dollars off my walk this morning"

Liz and Jessica were standing on the street corner with their hands on their hips. They had obviously been spying on Roxy and had heard the entire exchange between her and Matt.

"Didn't we discuss that Matt is off limits?" Liz asked curtly. "When will you ever learn?"

"Is Matt your personal property?" Roxy demanded. She was sick of being nice. She didn't care anymore how mean Liz could be. "I think he can speak for himself."

"I know that Matt didn't kiss you on purpose. I know that you made him do it because you were jealous," Liz sneered.

"Jealous of what?" Roxy asked.

Matt just stood there and stared at the ground. He didn't say a word. The silence was deafening until someone yelling in the distance caught everyone's attention.

"Roxy! Hey, Roxy! Wait up! Roooooxxxxyyyy!"

It was Kim and Georgia. Georgia had on a Mets baseball cap, black yoga pants, and a red T-shirt. She was walking Melody, a big, shaggy white dog that looked like a giant mop. Kim was right behind her, and Roxy could barely look at her ensemble.

Kim was wearing a stained T-shirt with a faded picture

of a Labrador retriever ironed onto it. A tool belt hung from her waist and held all her doggie supplies. To complete the look, a whistle—like the gym teacher's—dangled around Kim's neck. Roxy was dumbfounded. She wanted to pretend she didn't see Kim and Georgia, but it was too late.

"Roxy, what's going on here?" Georgia asked breathlessly as she ran over. Kim barely said hello. Instead, she dashed over to Chloe, stroked her head, and whispered in her ear. In less than thirty seconds, Chloe sat obediently for the first time all morning.

"I thought you guys were dog walkers, not plumbers!" Liz said while laughing hysterically at Kim's outfit. Jessica pulled out her phone and snapped a picture.

Kim pretended she couldn't hear and just continued to calm down the dogs. Roxy was sure she saw a flash of hurt cross Kim's face.

"Oh, so do our outfits not meet beauty-pageant standards?" Georgia lashed back. "Or sorry, my bad, did we forget to consult the Fashion Bible this morning?"

"That's it. You're walking my dog for *free* from now on," Liz insisted. "Insulting your clients? Wasting valuable time when you could have had little Roxie home by now? You're lucky I don't tell Principal West…and I can't promise I won't tweet about this incident unless my walks are on the house."

Roxy didn't move a muscle. She wanted to stand up to Liz. She wanted to defend Kim and Georgia. But she just couldn't get the words out.

"Well, then, I guess we agree. I'll bring little Roxie home

since it would take you another eight hours at this rate and it's almost time for school," Liz said as she grabbed little Roxie away from Kim. "This better not happen again."

Liz and Jessica headed toward the house. Roxy, Kim, Georgia, Matt, and the rest of the dogs just stood there and stared at each other in silence.

"Well, guys, I have to go," Matt said quietly. "I need to walk Banjo, but I'll ask my mom if you can start walking him. Roxy, I'll talk to you later?"

Roxy nodded and watched him run off.

"What was that all about?" Georgia asked. "Why were you so quiet? Nice of you to stand up for us!"

"I thought we were going to 'train her with kindness,'" Roxy cried. "And I'm sorry, but no more T-shirts with animal pictures, Kim!"

"Oh, I'm sorry that we don't follow Roxy's Rules when it comes to fashion, friends, or anything else for that matter," Georgia exclaimed. "I think that Kim can do whatever she wants and absolutely wear whatever she wants. We'd be lost without her."

"That's not true...there's no such thing as Roxy's Rules." Roxy felt tears start to well up in her eyes. She tried to fight them because the last thing she needed was for Georgia to think she was a crybaby on top of everything else she probably thought about her.

"No, but you still care way too much what that teen queen Liz Craft thinks about you," Georgia huffed. "Well, guess what? I don't care how many tiaras she has in her bedroom—she is not the ruler of the Doggy Divas! Right, Kim?"

Kim was silent for almost a full minute before she spoke. "Does it matter what I think? Liz is awful, but she could care less about me. I just want to walk dogs. In fact, I have a few notes about the way you two were handling your dogs for later..."

Roxy and Georgia tried to suppress their laughter. Leave it to Kim to care more about the dogs than their social status!

"Okay, guys, I have to take the rest of these dogs home so I can get to school." Roxy stood up and started untangling the dogs, with Kim's help. "I'm sorry—I really am, but let's just try to get past this. Liz wants us to fight, and we can't let her win. Let's catch up at lunch, okay?"

"Yeah, I'm sorry too," Georgia said. "I just don't like having Liz all up in our business."

"Just give it time," Roxy sighed. "Let's just try to stay positive until then."

DOGGY CONFESSIONAL
TYLER

Did Cupid come to town? First I have that little minx Chloe following me around with love-struck eyes. I've told her that I don't want anything serious. Girls! It's not that she isn't a cutie-pie, but I like to keep my options open. Commitment is definitely not for the weak at heart.

But what's the deal with my new dog walker, Roxy, and that jock Matt Billings who keeps hanging around? You can tell that Matt wants her to be his girlfriend, but I can smell the fear on him. In the dog world, you go after what you want. Fight or flight! If Matt likes Roxy, he's going to have to fight for her. If not, he should just let her go.

Humans! They're so complicated!

Chapter Eleven

ROXY RACED HOME FROM her dog-walking disaster, took the stairs two at a time to her room, and threw on a pair of black tights and the first oversized tunic that she saw hanging in her closet. She dabbed on a hint of mascara in a desperate attempt to make her eyes look brighter and less tired.

The Doggy Divas had been in business for two weeks, and Roxy wasn't sure how much longer she could handle waking up early to walk dogs, spending all day at school, coming home, walking even more dogs, and keeping up her grades. At least Principal West was allowing the Doggy Divas to get to school a few minutes late because the regular dog walkers were still on strike.

Roxy logged onto her laptop to quickly update the Doggy Diva Twitter feed before dashing out the door to meet her dad at the car.

@MissDoggyDiva: See you at lunch to book appointments, sell our super-sweet sweaters, and more!

Roxy then quickly attempted to repair the nail that the dogs had broken that morning by filing it down and plastering a thick coat of nail polish on it. The polished nail looked so thick and uneven that she just removed the polish from all of her nails. Roxy admitted nail defeat—there was no use trying to maintain a manicure around so many dogs.

Her laptop let out a little ring, announcing a response to her post!

@TIARALIZ: DDs are lame. Dogs peeing on my terrace = bad!

Roxy wanted to hit "Delete" and get rid of Liz's comment, but she decided to leave that up to a vote with the other two girls. After all, there were three VPs in this business.

"Roxy!" her dad called from the bottom of the stairs. "We're leaving now, or you're walking—your choice!"

Roxy ran a quick brush through her hair and glanced in the mirror. She dabbed more blush on each cheek.

Good enough! she thought as she ran down to the car. Roxy was way too tired for any more walking, so she needed to make sure she got a ride. Her dad was already in the driver's seat with the engine started.

Phew! Just in time!

Roxy got in the backseat, and her dad rolled his eyes. With a second thought, she threw open the door and jumped into the front seat next to him. He gave her a quick smile.

As soon as they pulled out of the driveway, Roxy's BlackBerry lit up with emails and texts from prospective clients.

She was so focused on reading and responding to every message that she didn't realize her dad was trying to talk to her.

"Earth to Roxy! Come in…earth to Roxy!" her dad laughed.

"Huh?" Roxy barely raised her head as she typed fast and furiously on the tiny keypad of her phone. "I have a lot of emails here. I'm sorry!"

"That's okay, Pumpkin," her dad said. "I was just saying that the neighborhood looks a lot better, and I'm proud of you for lending a hand. You must have gotten the business genes from your grandpa!"

"What are you talking about?" Roxy asked. She had known her parents would worry about her grades, ask way too many questions, and want to get involved.

"The Doggy Divas? Isn't that you?" her dad asked with a chuckle. "You could have told your mother and me. We're so proud of you for taking the initiative to help out the town!"

"How did you know? It wasn't a secret. I just wasn't sure what you and Mom would say…"

"I may seem like I was born in the 1800s, but I do log onto the Internet every now and then," her dad admitted. "I assume that Liz and little Roxie are a part of this too?"

"Well, not exactly," Roxy admitted. "I'm not sure that we'll be hanging out so much anymore. She's involved with her pageants, and I have this business…"

"Well, friendships do change. It's only natural to grow apart as you get older and develop new interests," her dad said. "I don't think that you should worry about it too much. It happens to the best of friends."

Roxy thought about her dad's words as she walked from his car to her locker.

It happens to the best of friends…but were Liz and I ever truly best friends?

Kim and Georgia were both waiting for her. Roxy was surprised at how happy and excited she was to see them.

I guess I've made some new friends after all!

Roxy couldn't help but notice that Kim was wearing a splash of perfume and a hint of clear lip gloss. That was a much needed improvement after her catastrophic outfit two weeks ago. Roxy decided she didn't want to embarrass Kim by calling attention to it, but she was impressed by the effort.

"I saw Liz's response to your tweet," Georgia said hurriedly. "I think we should keep it up there but respond with all the ways that she is a fake, a pageant fraud…maybe send an anonymous letter to the officials of her next pageant."

"And stoop to her level?" Roxy asked. "No. My email has been blowing up all morning with new business requests. I don't really think we have to worry. Liz can try all she wants to ruin this for us, but her attempts aren't working."

"I'm almost finished with my new treat recipe, so we can sell treats soon too," Kim said as she set down a bowl of water for a stray mutt roaming the halls. Dogs were still all over the school, even though technically Principal West had never allowed that beyond the one disastrous Bring Your Dog to School Day.

"With all this business, we'll have a lot to discuss at our meeting today!" Roxy declared. "I'll see you all at Georgia's after your last walk."

Roxy spent the rest of her day booking appointments and scheduling services. The Doggy Divas were still mini-celebrities at Monroe Middle School, and Roxy loved every minute of their newfound fame. It was way better than being co-ruler of the seventh grade with Liz. Roxy finally had a *real* say in her own life.

Roxy's after-school walks were a breeze compared to her past few morning walks. Chloe had gotten into the garbage during the day and, according to her owner, wasn't feeling well and needed to stay home. Roxy found the dogs much easier to manage without Chloe and Tyler running circles around her.

But the biggest relief was that Liz was at pageant training. Rosie, the Crafts' housekeeper—who barely spoke English—handed Roxy little Roxie and didn't say a word. Needless to say, Roxy was in a great mood when she knocked on the front door of the Sweeney house for the latest Doggy Diva meeting.

"Hello!" Georgia said with a smile as she swung the heavy oak door open. "Come in. Do you want a cup of coffee?"

Roxy only had a sip or two of coffee every now and then during breakfast when her parents weren't looking. The bittersweet taste wasn't exactly her most favorite thing. Roxy smelled a pot brewing as she followed Georgia into the kitchen. Kim was sitting at the table with Izzy, Dixie, and Jazzy curled up on her lap. The Chihuahuas were nipping at her untied shoelaces from their spot on the floor.

"You drink coffee?" Roxy asked. "I don't even know how to use the machine."

"I love coffee. My parents get home from work super-late and still have a ton of work to do, so I make it for them every night. I liked the smell so I started drinking it too." Georgia shrugged as she added cream and sugar to a cup, poured in the fresh brew, and handed the cup to Roxy. "Try it—I make the best coffee in Monroe County, according to my mom."

"I believe her," Roxy said as she pushed the piping-hot cup away with a giggle. "But, no thanks."

"I'm surprised Liz never made you hang out at trendy coffeehouses while sipping lattes and nibbling on scones," Georgia said as she sat down with the girls at the table. "I know how sophisticated Liz is supposed to be and all."

"Do we really have to bash Liz every five minutes?" Roxy asked. She wasn't defending Liz—she was just sick of always talking about her. "We have a lot of more important and way more interesting things to discuss."

"Well, sorry," Georgia said as she took Dixie from Kim and let the dog lap a few sips of coffee from her mug.

"Um, Georgia...coffee really isn't the best thing..." Kim interjected as she slid the cup away from Dixie's reach. Dixie whimpered and jumped off Georgia's lap and ran into the other room.

"I think we're doing so great—even with Liz trying to interfere with our success—that it really hasn't mattered,"

Roxy explained. "I know you don't like her. We should just let it be."

"Then can you just explain why you're here with us and not ruling the school with that tiara-wearing champ?" Georgia asked as she cupped her mug in both hands and took a slow sip. "I mean, the second you guys become BFFs again, the Doggy Divas is over, right?"

"Do you think you'll ever be friends again?" Kim asked with a bit of panic in her tone before Roxy could answer Georgia.

"I honestly don't know if we'll ever be friends again, but if we are, that definitely doesn't mean the end of the Doggy Divas," Roxy said. "Do you really think I would do that to you guys?"

"Well, let's be honest here—you and Liz didn't exactly help my social life blossom last year," Georgia said. "I wasn't trying to be the weird new girl that no one ever talked to."

"You weren't nice to me either," Kim said softly. "I mean, no one is ever really that nice to me...but you guys were the worst."

Roxy sank down in her seat and put her chin on the table. She knew that Kim and Georgia were right. She had wondered if they would confront her about this one day. She just hadn't thought that would happen so soon.

"Look, I apologize. I really do," Roxy said softly. "Liz and I had been best friends since elementary school, so I just always followed her lead. I guess I really didn't know any better or realize she wasn't very nice. I wanted to be popular. I'm starting to realize that maybe everyone didn't think we were so amazing after all."

"Liz is just really mean," Kim said. "She's what they would call the alpha dog. She's the leader, and the other dogs accept it whether they want to or not because they like having someone tell them what to do."

Georgia and Roxy burst out laughing.

"Kim, is there anything you can't relate back to something that has to do with dogs?" Roxy laughed. "How about this? Let's make a pact right now not to talk about Liz Craft anymore unless she has something to do with official Doggy Divas business?"

"Sounds like another one of Roxy's Rules to me. You got a lot of those!" Georgia said. "But I'm in. Liz gives me a headache. I think I have a Barbie doll that's more sincere and real than she'll ever be!"

Roxy smiled. Her cell phone started buzzing with a call from a number that she didn't recognize. She just assumed it was a new client.

"Doggy Divas, this is Roxy!" she chirped into the phone as she pulled out the appointment book. The schedule was so full that she hoped this was a client wanting to cancel a walk. "How may I help you?"

"Yes...hello, Roxy," an official-sounding voice replied. "This is Victoria Malone from Channel Two news. Do you have a moment?"

Roxy was sure that this had to be a prank phone call.

Victoria Malone knew about the Doggy Divas? Was this Liz disguising her voice?

Roxy couldn't believe the caller was really Victoria Malone. She watched Victoria every night. She did a segment called "Vic's Picks" about the coolest things going on around town. It was Roxy's favorite part of the nightly news.

"Why, yes, of course I have a moment," Roxy said in her most professional tone. "What can I do for you?"

"Well, Roxy, I've heard remarkable things about the Doggy Divas. Is it true that you and your partners are only in the seventh grade?" Victoria asked.

Roxy gulped. *Was it illegal for seventh graders to walk dogs?*

"Um, yes," Roxy said trying to keep her cool. "That's correct."

"That's very impressive. I'd love to do a segment on the Doggy Divas on 'Vic's Picks.' Would that be okay with you and your business partners?"

Roxy nodded her head vigorously but realized that Victoria couldn't see what she was doing through the phone. Kim and Georgia were making all sorts of faces and hand gestures as they desperately tried to figure out who Roxy was talking to.

"Oh, my God!" Roxy squealed. "*Yes!* We would love that!"

What would we love? Georgia mouthed. Roxy waved her hand in front of her face and tried to concentrate.

"Okay, I'll come by with a camera crew on Saturday afternoon and just follow you guys around as you do your thing," Victoria explained. "I'll have Sal from my office call you in a few minutes with the rest of the details. Thanks so much, Roxy. See you this weekend!"

Roxy hung up the phone in disbelief.

"Um, yo, Roxy! You going to tell us what that was all about?" Georgia asked. "What in the world is going on?"

"Are we in trouble for something?" Kim asked.

"Kim, it's okay! I promise you that we are absolutely *not* in trouble," Roxy stood on her chair for dramatic effect. "Ladies, I have big news. You're never going to believe who was on the phone!"

Georgia and Kim sat up straight.

"Well, come on," Georgia said. "Don't leave us hanging!"

Roxy took a deep breath.

"We're going to be on TV!" she shrieked. "That was Victoria Malone from 'Vic's Picks'! She wants to do an entire segment on the Doggy Divas!"

Georgia pulled Roxy down from the chair, and they started jumping and hugging and screaming all around Georgia's kitchen. All the dogs looked at them like they were crazy and dashed off into the other room.

"How did this happen?" Georgia asked breathlessly between high jumps. "She really cares about our dinky little dog-walking business?"

"That's exactly why she cares about us!" Roxy exclaimed excitedly. "How many seventh-grade entrepreneurs do *you* know that have cleaned up their town? We're like hometown heroes!"

Kim sat motionless in her chair. She twirled a Doggy-O around her finger. Her face was glum.

"What's the matter with you?" Georgia asked. "Get up here and celebrate with us!"

"Are you okay, Kim?" Roxy asked. "The dogs always come back out to play after they run off, and they really couldn't have gone very far if that's what you're worried about..."

"No, it's not that," Kim said quietly. "I'm fine. This is really exciting news."

Roxy and Georgia exchanged a concerned look and sat back down.

"What's wrong?" Roxy asked.

"You look like you're going to throw up," Georgia exclaimed. "And if you do, you better get to the bathroom now! My mom will kill me when she gets home and sees chunks on the kitchen floor..."

"I'm not going to throw up. At least I don't think so," Kim said quietly. "Guys, I can't be on TV!"

"Well, good thing there's no such thing as smell-o-vision yet," Georgia said. "I mean, your perfume today does help, but nothing beats a nice bubble bath..."

She stopped talking as soon as Roxy caught her eye with a look that clearly said, "Shut up."

"I mean, you'll be fine," Georgia promised. "We'll help you pick out an outfit and do your hair and make sure you shower if a bath isn't your cup of tea."

"Don't worry, Kim. We *all* have to figure out what we're going to wear." Roxy groaned as her cell phone buzzed again. "Doggy Divas, Roxy speaking."

"Yeah, hi there, Roxy," a gruff voice said. "This is Sal with Channel Two. We'll be filming you this Saturday for 'Vic's Picks,' all right?"

"Why, yes, of course, Sal," Roxy said sweetly. "We were expecting your call."

"I need you to email me all your addresses. We'll follow each of you around that morning as you go on your walks, and then Vic will chat with you girls at the dog park," Sal explained. "Expect us at ten."

"Okay, Sal. We can't wait," Roxy said as she bounced up and down. "We'll see you on Saturday."

Roxy snapped her phone shut and squealed with excitement. She whipped out her BlackBerry to update the Doggy Divas Twitter feed and Facebook page with the news while Georgia went to call her mom. Kim still sat there looking grim.

"Kim, you're in luck," Roxy declared. "We're going to give you a makeover."

"We are?" Georgia asked doubtfully when she walked back into the kitchen.

"You are?" Kim asked hopefully.

Roxy shot Georgia a pleading look.

"I mean...of course, we are!" Georgia corrected herself.

"I don't know. All your clothes are so, uh, sparkly," Kim said sadly. "And makeup makes my eyes twitch."

"Maybe it's the dog hair that makes your…" Georgia was cut off by Roxy again.

"Saturday morning, be at my house at 8 a.m. That will give us plenty of time to get you glamorous before the cameras come," Roxy said. "Georgia and I will make you look beautiful—I promise! Just think of it as another one of Roxy's Rules!"

"I'm going to throw up," Kim said. "I can't do this."

"No throwing up!" Roxy insisted. "Everyone go home and email your clients that a camera crew will be with you on Saturday afternoon. And get some rest—we can't have circles under our eyes on camera!"

"You do realize that you're going to have to email Liz about this, right?" Georgia asked. "Let's just start preparing now. She's going to steal the spotlight for herself!"

Of course she will. Roxy gulped.

"I'll handle it," she said. "I'll just email her like I would any other client and not make it such a big deal."

And, of course, that's way easier said than done…

DOGGY CONFESSIONAL
IZZY

We're going to be on TV? Did Kim freak out? I hope Kim gives us one of her splendid spa days to make sure we're camera ready! And it wouldn't hurt if Kim treated herself to something nice and sweet smelling too. She deserves it. She spends so much time taking care of us that she forgets about herself. Now that's a true friend.

Chapter Twelve

THE WEEK FLEW BY so fast that Saturday arrived before Roxy was ready. Everyone at school had heard that the Doggy Divas were going to be on "Vic's Picks" and wanted to book their dog walks for Saturday so they could be on TV too. The girls decided that the only way to keep things fair was to give clients with standing Saturday appointments first dibs. But the girls did send out a mass email to all their clients so they could cheer the Doggy Divas on at the park during the interview.

Unfortunately, little Roxie was already on the schedule for Saturday afternoon. Roxy hoped that Liz had a baton-twirling lesson or something to keep her away. But that hope was dashed when Roxy received an email response from Liz that simply said:

Roxy,

Since I'll have to get little Roxie groomed and bathed for this opportunity, I assume that means you'll be adding more free walks to my account to cover those costs. I know the Doggy Divas offer grooming, but my Roxie's fur can only be washed by Bruno at Pooch Palace, so you'll have to cover that expense. We'll see you on Saturday.

Liz

Roxy was upset that Liz had just signed her name. Usually their emails ended with "xoxoxoxo to infinity" or "Love, your best friend in the world." It was just another reminder that their friendship was done. Roxy felt uneasy as she started pulling out makeup, hair products, and possible outfits to wear. She wasn't convinced that Liz would stay so cordial once the cameras started rolling. Last year, Liz had written an essay in English class about how her five-year plan included starring on a reality TV show.

The doorbell rang, and Roxy looked out her bedroom window. Georgia and Kim stood on the porch bursting with nervous energy. The plan was to get ready together— give Kim her makeover—and then head home to wait for their assigned cameramen. Roxy's mom answered the door. When Roxy ran downstairs, her mom was talking a mile a minute to Kim and Georgia about how proud she was of the Doggy Divas.

"You girls are an inspiration!" Roxy's mom gushed. "I always knew my Roxy was talented, but this is beyond what I thought she would accomplish…"

"Okay, Mom, that's enough," Roxy said as she grabbed Kim and Georgia by the hands and dragged the girls up the stairs. "We're very busy…"

"Wow, your mom is really impressed that we're going to be on TV, huh?" Georgia asked as they settled into Roxy's room. Georgia dumped out a bag of hair accessories and costume jewelry onto Roxy's bed.

"Aren't your parents?" Roxy asked as she started

brushing the knots out of Kim's hair. Kim actually handed her a dog brush, and Roxy didn't argue. She needed those heavy-duty bristles to get through Kim's frizzy mane. Roxy was afraid to ask Kim when she'd brushed her hair last.

"They're proud of me, but they're working today—like they do every weekend," Georgia said as she started filing Kim's nails. "They were gone before I woke up this morning."

"I didn't even tell my mom," Kim said as she closed her eyes so Roxy could curl her eyelashes. "She would have wanted to make me over herself. It's like her dream to have a spa day with me. But I knew that as soon as I mentioned the word 'dog,' I'd lose her attention."

"Well, I think she'll be very impressed with how you look," Roxy said as she applied some mascara on her own lashes and then dabbed a bit onto Kim's. "Don't open your eyes, or you'll have globs all over your face!"

"It burns!" Kim cried as her eyes started watering.

"Um, okay, so I think we're good with the mascara, and we're just going to skip the eyeliner," Roxy said as she handed Kim some deodorant.

Georgia ran a flat iron through select strands of Kim's hair. Now that it was brushed and untangled, Kim's hair was almost too fine to hold the style Georgia was working on, but she didn't give up.

"*Owwwwww!*" Kim screamed. The iron slipped from Georgia's hands and burned Kim's wrist. "Okay, enough!"

"I'm sorry, Kim. I really am. But it hurts to be beautiful!" Georgia laughed. "We're almost done. Roxy, what color eye shadow do you think would look best with Kim's complexion?"

"I think gold or green. Or maybe green on the lids and gold on the brow?" Roxy answered as she pulled out a tight, off-the-shoulder cream-colored sweater that she thought would be perfect for Kim. She paired it with a pair of skinny jeans and her lavender Uggs. "Kim, you have the perfect face for makeup!"

"I have no idea what that means, but I feel like a science experiment!" Kim laughed as Roxy handed her the sweater and jeans to put on. Kim slipped into the Uggs, and Roxy dabbed light-pink lip gloss on Kim's lips while Georgia spritzed Kim with some light, flowery perfume.

"Are you ready for your big reveal?" Roxy asked as she and Georgia ushered Kim over to the mirror.

"I guess so," Kim said slowly. "My eyes are itching, and my face feels stiff. And this isn't really an outfit that will let me run after the dogs…"

"Whatever you do, do not touch your face or rub your eyes!" Roxy demanded. "You're like a work of art—and you wouldn't scribble all over a fresh painting, now would you?"

"You can suck up the outfit for one day. Tomorrow you can go back to tool belts and faded tees!" Georgia announced. "Okay, Kim, close your eyes. I think you're going to like what you see!"

Kim squeezed her eyes shut as Roxy and Georgia

positioned her in front of the mirror. "Okay, now!" Roxy and Georgia sang in unison.

Kim's eyes flew open. She was shocked at first, but then she started twirling around and posing in front of the mirror. "Is this really me?" she asked. "I feel like Madonna or something!"

Roxy and Georgia high-fived each other. Kim looked like a totally different person. Her lifeless brown hair now had shine and body to it. Her face, which was usually covered with dirt, was vibrant with just enough makeup to look natural. And no one had realized that Kim had such a tiny waist hiding beneath those frumpy T-shirts. The sweater showed off her model-esque frame.

"Okay. You guys have to get home. We have less than an hour until the camera crews show up at our houses!" Roxy said. "Kim, be careful. Do not eat anything. Do not touch your face. And do *not* let the dogs near your clothes!"

"Another one of Roxy's Rules?" Kim laughed as the girls gave each other a quick hug and ran out the door.

About thirty minutes later, Roxy let a grumpy, overweight cameraman named Bobby into her house. He smelled like coffee; his stomach peeked out from under his white T-shirt; and he called Roxy "sweetheart." She felt really weird when he followed her into the bathroom while she brushed her teeth—especially when he asked her to do it again.

"Don't spit in the sink so many times, sweetheart," he told her.

Roxy didn't understand what this had to do with dog walking, but she went along with it. Her parents kept a watchful eye from downstairs, but Roxy saw their faces beaming with pride. She wondered how the other girls' shoots were going as she grabbed her canine kit and led Bobby out the door and on the way to the first house.

"Great, sweetheart," Bobby said as he zoomed in on the kit. "Just keep smiling."

Bobby followed Roxy on her usual route. First, she picked up Horton, who barked incessantly at Bobby's camera. It took five treats to finally get the corgi to calm down. Then she picked up Precious, who ran into the street to chase a cat—with Horton flying after her. Roxy went tumbling down, and Bobby had to help her up. He made Roxy put Precious back in the house, knock on the door, and pick her up all over again.

Surprisingly, Chloe and Tyler were on their best behavior. They were intimidated by Bobby's deep voice and curious about the large camera looming over them. Then the moment Roxy dreaded arrived. It was time to pick up little Roxie.

"What's the matter?" Bobby asked. "At every other house, you skipped right up to the door with a big smile on your face. Does this dog bite or something?"

Roxy tried really hard to think of a good answer in case it was shown on TV.

"Well," Roxy laughed nervously, "the dog doesn't bite, but I'm not so sure about the owner."

Bobby raised his eyebrows and watched Roxy knock on the door. Liz opened the door with little Roxie in her arms and a big, welcoming smile plastered on her face.

"Roxy! Come in." Liz gave her a big hug. She shook Bobby's hand and batted her eyelashes. "We're so excited to get little Roxie on TV!"

Roxy looked around to make sure they were at the right house. What was going on here?

"Roxy and I have been best friends for years. Right, Rox?" Liz cooed to Bobby. "It was just a cool little coincidence that my dog was named Roxie too. It was meant to be, I guess."

Roxy was so nervous that she thought she would throw up all over Liz's pink leather loafers—the same loafers that Liz hadn't let Roxy buy at the mall over the summer because she claimed they were "last season." And she was calling her Rox? They were back on a nickname basis?

"I just gave my little Roxie a very special treat in honor of her TV debut," Liz said as she handed over little Roxie. "Have fun!"

Roxy gulped. This sounded awfully suspicious. Little Roxie was bouncing around more than usual.

What's going on? Roxy started to panic.

"You got it, sweetheart," Bobby said to Liz. "We'll be interviewing all the girls at the dog park, so be sure to meet us over there to cheer on your best friend."

Roxy was so worried that something was going on with little Roxie that she didn't even hear what Bobby instructed her to do next.

"I wouldn't miss it for the world!" Liz said brightly as Bobby, Roxy, and little Roxie made their way out of the house. "See you there!"

DOGGY CONFESSIONAL
LITTLE ROXIE

I guess Liz changed her mind and decided to be friends with Roxy again. She was in a terrific mood this morning, and she gave me a special new treat to drink called Pet Power. Liz said it would make me want to run around for hours! But whoa! I feel really happy now...like I've taken years off my life. I have the energy of a nine-month-old puppy! Look out, world—here I come!

Chapter Thirteen

ROXY LOOKED DOWN AT the black-and-tan overly excited pup with wide eyes. She was squirming and panting and wriggling. And her little head bounced around like a balloon filled with helium. Little Roxie was out of control. When Roxy stole a glance at Bobby, he looked equally worried. Unfortunately, his camera didn't stop rolling.

Roxy was doomed. The audience would think that the Doggy Divas were inexperienced and careless with their pets. This was going to ruin them.

"You always have this much trouble commanding these pooches?" Bobby asked as they walked toward the dog park. "I can't get a good angle with little Roxie shaking so much in your arms."

"Oh, no, little Roxie is just a little nervous about the cameras," Roxy gulped as she finally set the tiny dog down on the sidewalk. "I'm sure she'll calm down as soon as we start walking."

But the second little Roxie's paws touched the sidewalk, she broke free and tore away. It happened so fast! Roxy just stood there absolutely stunned. Luckily, she'd remembered to grip the other dogs' leashes as tightly as possible.

"Honey, that little dog looked like she was on speed or something," Bobby said worriedly. "We need to go look for her."

Tears welled in Roxy's eyes as she broke into a run.

As Roxy got closer to the dog park, she heard a huge commotion. People were talking excitedly, and dogs were barking. Roxy spotted Kim and Georgia inside the park's dog run—a big, grassy patch enclosed by a fence.

Dogs were running free, playing fetch, and catching Frisbees. Other dog owners stood around the fence holding up posters that cheered on their dogs and said "We Love The Doggy Divas!" Victoria Malone was right in the center of it all. She was shuffling through a stack of index cards while talking on her cell phone.

Roxy had no choice but to take the dogs she did have over to Kim and Georgia in the center of the park.

"Girls," Roxy whispered urgently. "We have a big problem!"

Roxy's heart sunk when she saw Liz standing on the sidelines with Jessica.

"No problems here. Look at this crowd!" Georgia said with a big smile. She and Dixie were wearing matching yellow sweaters. "Vic will be off the phone in a minute…"

"I lost little Roxie!" Roxy whispered back. "She was totally hyper and ran off the second I put her down. It's not like her!"

"It sounds like Liz gave her Pet Power. It's this fancy new energy drinks for dogs!" Kim cried. "It's totally safe except she might crash a little when it starts to wear off. I don't think Liz read the label carefully…"

"Okay…we don't have time for that now." Roxy was panicking. "How do we find little Roxie before Liz or Vic notices?"

"Why don't you get your boyfriend to help you?" Georgia said with a smile as she nodded over to the crowd.

Roxy turned to see Matt standing just outside the fence and beaming with pride. He waved and gave her a thumbs-up. Roxy blushed. But before they could do anything, Victoria snapped her cell phone shut and turned to face the girls.

"You must be Roxy!" Victoria clasped her perfectly manicured hand over Roxy's like they were long-lost friends. Victoria was taller in person, and her mane of curly red hair looked like a blaze of fire as it glistened in the sun. She spoke each word perfectly, as if she was always reading from a teleprompter. "I'm delighted to meet you."

"Me too. Thank you so much for featuring us!" Roxy said nervously. She kept looking around and hoping that Liz's puppy had found her way back.

"Now, which one is little Roxie?" Victoria asked sweetly. "I just met her owner, Liz. She told me that you guys are best friends. Is that right? I thought it would be fun to include an interview with Liz about how proud she is of her best friend!"

Roxy dug her feet into the ground.

"Excuse me. I don't mean to interrupt, but where is my dog?" Liz's shrill voice pierced Roxy's ears. "I see all these dogs with you and no little Roxie."

Liz's hands were planted fiercely on her hips. The camera, of course, was pointed right at them.

"You're, uh, missing a dog, dear?" Victoria looked disappointed as she cautiously eyed the camera. "Has this happened before? I thought you girls were responsible. That's why we're dedicating a whole segment to the Doggy Divas."

"I'll call the police and tell them you are a thief, Roxy Davis, if you don't find my dog in five minutes!" Liz shrieked.

The park went dead silent.

"We're going to find her. Just calm down," Roxy pleaded. "You're the one who gave her some kind of doggy energy drink to make her too hyper to listen to me."

"I did no such thing!" Liz exclaimed. "I would never be so irresponsible…unlike you and your little team of so-called divas here."

"Kim, isn't there anything you can do to help us find little Roxie?" Roxy pleaded.

Liz had a look of pure evil on her face. Victoria's mouth was twisted into a wry smile as she watched the scene unfold. Roxy couldn't help but notice that she kept holding the microphones closer to them and never told the cameras to stop rolling.

I guess that's show biz for you! Roxy thought as she waited for Kim to work her doggy magic.

"Kim is the dog expert and trainer of the Doggy Divas," Georgia explained. "C'mon, Kim, tell us how you can get a hyper dog to come back."

The crowd was getting very anxious, and some of the dog owners requested that the Doggy Divas give them back their beloved pets.

"Well, if little Roxie did drink Pet Power this morning… I'd guess by now it's worn off and she's worn out," Kim said slowly. "I'll bet she just found a place to sleep and will find her way home when she wakes up."

"I want my dog," Liz demanded. "My dad is a lawyer, and we will sue you if you don't find my dog right now."

"I'm sorry, girls, but this is not what we were expecting," Victoria said. "We spent a lot of time getting the crews together, and finding out that you lost a dog is just unacceptable. I'd hate to have to make this a piece about why your business is a failure."

In that moment, Roxy wished that Liz had never gone to pageant camp and that Matt had never asked her to hang out. If those two things had never happened, she wouldn't be in this mess right now. And why did Jessica seem to be talking to her tote bag?

Without hesitating, Roxy whispered something to Kim, who didn't miss a beat. She let out a piercing, high-pitched whistle that made all the dogs in the park stand at attention, ears pointed up, as if awaiting their next command. That included the little dog in Jessica's oversized bag. Startled, Jessica dropped the bag, and little Roxie came tumbling out, looking a little dazed.

"Roxie! There you are!" Liz squealed. "I was so worried about you."

"Excuse me, but didn't the dog just come out of your friend's bag?" Victoria asked skeptically.

For the first time that Roxy could remember, Liz was speechless.

"I'm sorry, Liz. I thought the bag was closed," Jessica stuttered. "I was trying to get out of here to get her home, but with all these people and dogs and whistling…"

"So you stole your own dog?" Victoria asked. "Do I have this right?"

Little Roxie was so excited to be released from the bag that she raised her tiny leg and let out a long stream of pee that dribbled onto Jessica's pricey bag and sandals. Kim, Roxy, and Georgia burst out laughing.

"This is a $200 bag, and these are my mom's shoes. She doesn't know I'm wearing them!" Jessica cried. "I knew this was a stupid idea. Who gives their own dog Pet Power and then dog-naps it?"

Jessica held her bag as far away from her body as possible and stomped off. Liz stood there holding little Roxie and with a stunned smile on her face.

"Little Roxie is confused from all the excitement," Kim said with concern as she pulled a portable bowl out of her bag and filled it with water. "Put her down so she can drink."

The little dog lapped up the water faster than Kim could pour it into the bowl.

"Now, Liz…is that your name? I suggest that you get out of here so I can interview the Doggy Divas," Victoria said coldly. Liz swallowed so hard that everyone in earshot heard her.

"And I think I just may call Principal West later today. He's an old friend of mine. He mentioned that you participate in pageants. Being a former beauty queen myself, I'm friends with many of the pageant commissioners across the country. And I can assure you, this is no way for a queen to behave."

Liz nodded as she backed away. Roxy was sure she saw a tear start to slide down Liz's cheek.

"I don't know how many more crowns you'll be earning," Victoria said.

"This isn't over, Roxy," Liz hissed as she brushed past her and stopped in front of Matt. Roxy hadn't even realized that he was still standing there.

"Are you coming with me or staying in Loserville?" Liz asked him.

"I think you need to head home," Matt said with his arms crossed. "I didn't think even you would stoop low enough to hide your own dog. Come to think of it, I think Victoria would be very interested in hearing about how you blackmailed me into being your boyfriend."

"I didn't..." Liz started to say, but she thought better of it with everyone watching. She grabbed little Roxie and stomped out of the park.

"Girls, I'm so sorry. I have to get to my next interview, so I can't finish your segment today. But we will make this up to you, I promise," Victoria said sincerely. "Those antics may help Liz win pageants, but I don't have the patience for them. And I have your card, so I'll call you to start walking my Akita, Barbie Walters."

The girls squealed with delight as Victoria walked away.

"Our first celebrity client!" Roxy said, jumping up and down. "Victoria Malone is our client!"

They huddled together for a group hug while Izzy, Dixie, and the Chihuahuas bounced all around them.

"I can't believe that after all we did, Liz still succeeded in screwing up our TV debut," Roxy said. "I mean, I know Victoria is going to re-interview us, especially after we show her our dog-walking skills, but still…"

Georgia and Kim smiled.

"I think this all worked out," Georgia said. "Finally someone set Liz straight—at least for now!"

"Someone needs to call Animal Control on her," Kim said angrily. "She dog-napped her own dog! Is she insane?"

The girls burst out laughing and fell into a group hug. Roxy felt a tap on her back and broke free from the squeeze. Matt Billings and Banjo were standing behind her.

Kim and Georgia slowly started to collect the dogs and walk away.

"Hey! Where are you guys going?" Roxy asked while staring right into Matt's soft brown eyes and smiling at him.

"Um, I think I just made up something new to add to Roxy's Rules," Georgia laughed. "When you get that dreamy look on your face around Matt, Kim and I will bolt!"

"Yeah—have fun!" Kim said as they ran off.

Could they embarrass me any more if they tried?

"Hey," Matt said quietly. "I'm really sorry about today."

Roxy's heart was pounding.

"Why are you sorry?" she asked. "You didn't do anything."

He bit his lip.

"No, but I knew something was up when Liz started telling Victoria that you guys were the best friends ever." His eyes clouded over. "I saw her and Jessica whispering as soon they got here. And they were treating Jessica's bag like it had gold inside. But I never expected little Roxie to be in there. I can't believe I was so scared of her telling Coach lies about me that I let it ruin things between us. This is my fault."

"It's not your fault," Roxy said. And she meant it. "Liz finally got what was coming to her. Liz Craft is a fraud."

Matt breathed a sigh of relief.

"Oh, good!" he said. "I've really been a wreck over this whole nightmare."

"Well," Roxy said. "You're not off the hook yet. You still have to make it up to me."

"Is that what the girls mean by Roxy's Rules?" he whispered in her ear. "Is making it up to you a new rule?"

Before Roxy could answer, Matt leaned down and gave her a soft kiss right on her lips. He smiled at her and grabbed her hand.

"I have to get to baseball practice, but I'll see you at school on Monday!"

Roxy held the hand he'd just touched to the exact spot on her lips where he'd kissed her and watched him run away.

So, it looks like seventh grade will rule after all!

DOGGY CONFESSIONAL
CHLOE

Finally, those two kissed! Now Matt just needs to take Roxy out on a proper date...but puppy steps! Maybe Tyler will get the knot out of his tail and finally ask *me* out. At least we'll have our walks with the Doggy Divas!

Coming Soon...

THE Doggy Divas

LIGHTS, CAMERA, KIM

"Izzy—sit!" Kim Pierce commanded to her hyper Maltese. She was desperately trying to paint Izzy's tiny claws with hot pink doggy nail polish. She just returned from a shopping spree at the pet store with her friend and business partner, Roxy Davis. They were sitting in Kim's backyard trying to enjoy the last hour of sunshine on an unusually warm late fall afternoon.

"If we can get crazy Izzy to sit for a manicure—we can get any dog to do it! Just imagine what that will do for business!" Roxy said with a sparkle in her eye while typing on her Blackberry with one finger. "Georgia, why don't you try out the silver glittery shade on Dixie's nails?"

Dixie was Georgia's docile miniature dachshund, and Georgia was the third business partner in the Doggy Divas. It was a full-service doggy walking, training, grooming, and fashion-consulting company that the three seventh graders started just three short months before. On the first day of school, all the dog walkers in town had gone on strike, leaving their town a mess and dogs roaming the streets—and Monroe Middle School. The girls, an unlikely trio at first, formed the Doggy Divas that became a rousing success with their unique offerings. They were now the top canine caregivers in town.

"Ugh, do I have to?" Georgia rolled her eyes. "I know we're going to get more nail polish on our clothes than we will on the dogs. Kim, you of all people really can't be an advocate of treating our pooches like Makeover Barbie, right?"

"Well, I looked at the ingredients on the bottle and this one's a totally natural and safe product, so I don't see the harm," Kim said with an air of authority. She *was* the dog expert of the group. "I mean, I wouldn't put it on a dog that doesn't like it, and we should probably keep this service strictly to girl dogs…"

"In business, we have to keep offering new things!" Roxy interrupted without looking up from her Blackberry. "I heard my dad tell a client once that if you get too predictable, your customers will get bored and move on!"

Roxy was the unofficial leader of the Doggy Divas. She was supposed to be the co-queen of the seventh grade except she had had a huge falling out with her now former best friend, Liz Craft. Roxy had kissed Liz's crush, Matt Billings, during the summer when Liz was away at pageant camp, and, well, that was enough for Liz to push Roxy out of the throne for good.

"In business, you can also fail," Georgia snapped. "And I don't see you trying to get a dog to sit still long enough to make it look like Paris Hilton! All you care about is Matt texting you. That's why you haven't looked up once all afternoon!"

Roxy's Blackberry let out a little jingle to alert her that she had a new text. Roxy blushed and immediately started typing on the tiny keyboard. Georgia's face turned egg-plant purple and Kim was sure that steam was going to blow from Georgia's ears.

"Excuse me for having a life!" Roxy finally retorted. "Besides, Matt was just texting that he agrees that doggy manicures would make us stand out…"

"Do you really need to send Matt a play-by-play of everything that happens when you're apart? He's not even officially…" Georgia trailed off. She had a bad habit of speaking before thinking.

"Not what? My boyfriend?" Roxy asked, her bright eyes clouding over as she slammed her Blackberry into its case. "I can still ask him for his opinion. His dog, Banjo, is one of our clients so…"

Georgia kept her head down and started clacking her needles together while a tiny doggy sweater started to take shape within seconds. Her designs were a hot seller for the Doggy Divas and it never ceased to amaze the girls how fast Georgia could create something right before their very eyes.

"I'm sorry," Georgia mumbled. "I didn't mean it like that."

"We're just taking things slow," Roxy said quietly.

"Is that what he told you?" Georgia asked. "I watch a lot of Oprah and she's big on communication in relationships…"

"No, we haven't had a big talk or anything, but we

161

know everything that's going on in each other's lives," Roxy chewed the bottom of her lip. "We're basically boyfriend and girlfriend just without the title. I mean, really, do we need to put a label on things?"

Georgia snorted and concentrated on her sweater. Roxy quietly typed on her Blackberry.

"Do you think he's afraid of what Liz will say if you have a title?" Kim asked while trying to force Izzy to sit in her lap. "She loves having the spotlight all to herself. If Matt refers to you as his girlfriend, that would set her off like a rocket!"

"Matt is not afraid of Liz and neither are any of us!" Roxy said angrily. She slammed her hand against the fence, and Georgia's knitting needles fell to the ground.

"I'm sorry," Roxy said in a softer tone. "The Liz drama was so three months ago. No one needs to worry about Liz—not me, not you guys, and definitely not Matt."

"Yes, Ma'am!" Georgia rolled her eyes and gave Roxy a salute.

"Look, Liz tried to sabotage the Doggy Divas and it didn't work, and she tried to blackmail Matt into being her boyfriend and that didn't work; so obviously we don't need to worry," Roxy said while absentmindedly painting her thumb over and over with a coat of the doggy nail polish. "Hey, this stuff isn't so bad! Georgia, why don't you try it on Dixie again?"

"This doggy nail polish idea is even more ridiculous than Liz's tiara collection," Georgia grumbled.

The girls were silent.

"Okay, it's been a long day and we all had to walk dogs for hours this morning so maybe we just need to go home and rest," Kim said, trying to take some control. "But we should talk about whether or not we want to start offering doggy manicures at our meeting next week—so we can vote and agree as a group!"

Kim was afraid of how the girls would respond so she focused on dabbing tiny dots of polish onto Izzy's nails without getting it all over the dog's black fur.

"I agree with Kim," Roxy said even though she was half paying attention.

"Me too," Georgia said while banging her knitting needles together. The sweater she had started creating just minutes before was almost complete. The beauty of making dog sweaters was that they were so tiny so they took no time and very little yarn to make.

"Good," Kim said softly.

Roxy and Georgia had been butting heads a lot recently. Kim didn't want to get involved but sometimes she worried if she didn't, one of these spats would become the end of the Doggy Divas. Kim knew that Roxy and Georgia cared about their business. But deep down Kim feared that without the Doggy Divas, the girls would no longer stay friends.

"Maybe we could treat *ourselves* to manicures one day too?" Georgia asked. "We work hard and we deserve it. Let's add that to next week's agenda."

"Now you're talking!" Roxy said with a smile. A phone rang and Roxy jumped up and scrambled to locate her phone. She had a sheepish look on her face when she realized it was Kim's phone ringing and sat back down.

"Don't worry!" Georgia exclaimed. "Maybe it *is* Matt. He could be asking Kim to help plan a surprise romantic date for you."

Roxy opened her mouth to say something but just glared at Georgia instead.

"I don't recognize the number," Kim said. She shrugged and answered it anyway. "Doggy Divas, this is Kim."

Kim's eyes became very wide. She didn't say much but listened intently. Roxy and Georgia kept mouthing to Kim to tell them who it was, but Kim did her best to ignore them.

"Yes, my business partners are right here," Kim said. "Sure, I can put you on speaker. Just give me a moment."

Kim covered the receiver of her cell phone with her hand. She was shaking with excitement. "Girls!" she whispered. "It's some guy who calls himself Tony the Tiger. He's heading up Posh Pets, the new pet division of the Hot Shots Talent Agency! He wants to have a meeting with us!"

Roxy and Georgia screamed in a whisper and gathered around Kim's phone. Kim pushed the speaker phone on, and they grabbed each other's hands.

"Hi, Tony, er, the Tiger," Kim said as the other girls tried not to giggle. "I have Roxy Davis and Georgia Sweeny with me on speaker phone."

"Hi!" Roxy and Georgia sang in unison.

"Do we call you Tony? Or Tony the Tiger?" Roxy asked. "Or Mr. Tiger?"

"Calling me Tony is just fine," he chuckled. "I've heard a lot about you girls. Everyone raves that you know all the best dogs in town, and I'd love for you to come in and tell me all about the Doggy Divas. Maybe you can help me sign some great new canine talent too. How does that sound?"

Roxy, Kim, and Georgia squeezed hands in excitement.

"Yes, Tony," Roxy jumped in. "We'd love to meet with you. Just tell us when and we'll be there."

"How about Monday afternoon after you're finished walking your dogs?" he asked.

"We'll be there!" Roxy exclaimed while nodding at the girls.

Kim hung up the phone in shock. "We don't have to be on TV again, right?" she asked. A few months ago the Doggy Divas were asked to be featured on a special segment of the news called Vic's Picks hosted by reporter Victoria Malone. Much to Kim's dismay, she was given a makeover for the taping. "My face still itches from all the make-up you made me wear for the Vic's Picks shoot!"

"We'll have to tell Victoria about this when we walk Barbie Walters next week!" Roxy exclaimed. Vic's Akita, Barbie Walters, was their most famous client.

"Roxy, you didn't even let me get a word in!" Georgia cried as she stood up and started throwing her knitting supplies into her bag. "Kim was the one that got the call, and you just took over. You're not the president of Doggy Divas. We all have vice-president titles in case you forgot."

"Georgia, what is the matter with you?" Roxy huffed. "We were all on the call *together*, I didn't realize only Kim was allowed to talk!"

"Guys, can we just stop this?" Kim pleaded. "He wanted to talk to *all* of us. We can't go to this meeting and fight in front of Tony."

Roxy's Blackberry jingled again. The girls just stood there looking at each other. Kim wondered who would be first to speak.

"Just get it," Georgia said flatly as she collected Dixie and the rest of her things. "I don't care if you text with Matt until your fingers fall off. I have stuff to take care of at home. I'll see you guys Monday."

Kim shut the gate to her backyard behind Georgia and turned around to find Roxy typing a mile a minute on her Blackberry. Kim sighed. She just wasn't comfortable being the peace-keeper of the group.

How would I train two dogs that weren't getting along? Kim wondered as she gave Izzy a treat.

"Are you taking off too?" Kim asked Roxy.

There was no response—just the sound of Roxy giggling and keys tapping.

"Roxy? Earth to Roxy!" Kim said and threw a treat at her.

"Huh?" Roxy looked confused. "Oh, sorry—Matt

just said the funniest thing about his baseball practice today…"

Kim shook her head.

"Okay, I'm going to go home," Roxy said without looking up. "Monday is going to be a big day, so rest up!"

"Are you and Georgia going to be okay?" Kim asked.

"Of course—she's just shooting off her mouth without thinking like always," Roxy said as she bent down to pet Izzy good-bye. "I know she doesn't mean it."

Kim sighed as she shut the gate behind Roxy. She was relieved that Roxy didn't seem too worried about arguing with Georgia. But Kim still couldn't help but fear that Roxy's obsessing over Matt and Georgia's new attitude problem could ruin the Doggy Divas and her first chance at real best friends—with two legs instead of four!